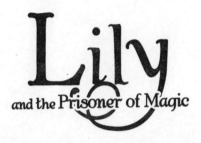

Lily
and the Prisoner of Magic

'There's something wrong. I don't know what it is, but the spells inside me are – are moving.' Georgie had her arms wrapped tightly around her chest, as though she was trying to hold something in. 'I think something's calling them.'

'The magic in the house?' Lily asked, frowning. She couldn't imagine how something that felt so gentle and essentially good under her fingers could be stirring up Mama's dark spells.

'No... I'm not sure...' Georgie gasped suddenly, and she sank down into a little huddle on the steps. 'Oh, it hurts!'

Lily

and the Prisoner of Magic

HOLLY WEBB

ORCHARD

ORCHARD BOOKS
338 Euston Road, London NW1 3BH
Orchard Books Australia
Level 17/207 Kent Street, Sydney, NSW 2000

First published in 2012 by Orchard Books

A Paperback Original

ISBN 978 1 40831 351 0

Text © Holly Webb 2012

A CIP catalogue record for this book is available from the British Library.

3 5 7 9 10 8 6 4 2

Printed in Great Britain

Orchard Books is a division of Hachette Children's Books,
an Hachette UK company.

www.hachette.co.uk

ONE

'No one's following us?' Lily asked, a little anxiously, peering back over her shoulder, as Fell Hall disappeared behind a row of softly curving hills.

The steady beat of the dragon's wings didn't slacken, even though he turned his great head to answer her. 'Were you expecting them to?'

He sounded as though he was smiling, she thought. Lily had only known him a few days, and she wasn't sure if dragons could actually smile. His mouth was probably the wrong shape – or perhaps he simply had too many teeth. 'No. No, I suppose not.' She stared down at the hills below them. They were so high up that the landscape looked like a picture in a book, dotted with delicate lines of hedges and roads.

Unconsciously, she tightened her grip on the dragon's scales.

'Only a dragon could fly this high, this fast,' the silvery dragon assured her. Then he was silent for a moment, and this time his wings did seem to falter a little, and Lily saw them lose a little height. The dragon had to beat his wings harder to bring them surging up again.

'What is it?' Lily asked him anxiously, once he was flying steadily again.

'I had not thought... The length of time we have been – away. Many things may have changed. Are there other things that fly?' His glittering black eyes fixed on hers, painfully wide.

'Not like you.' Lily shook her head. 'Nothing like you. I was being stupid; I can't make myself not be frightened of Miss Merganser, and the others at Fell Hall. But they didn't have spells for flying, I'm certain of it.'

'After what they did to you – and to your friends – being frightened is nothing to be ashamed of, Lily dear.' The tiny old lady squashed up behind Lily hugged her tightly, and Lily had to try not to laugh. She'd never imagined being hugged by a princess, even if Princess Jane was disgraced, and supposedly dead. She patted the thin, white-skinned hands around her waist gratefully.

'I shall fly faster,' the dragon said firmly. 'They must not catch up with us, and when it gets a little later, we shall have to put down and hide, of course. Too many towns to avoid on the way to London, or at least there always were.'

'There are more now, I should think,' Lily told him doubtfully. The dragon had last flown in the sixteenth century, and she suspected that back then even London had been rather small.

'Of course, of course,' he muttered, giving a little shiver of anticipation. She could feel excitement and magic shimmering through his scales. 'So much to see. We must get well ahead now. I shall not be able to talk for a while, Lily.'

The great silver-white wings beat down heavily, and Lily gasped as they lifted even higher in the air.

'Hold on!' she called back to the others.

'We already are!' her sister screamed back to her, the words half carried away on the wind. Georgie looked as though she had practically stuck herself to the dragon's ragged spines, she was clinging on so tight. Her light hair was streaming out behind her, and she looked like a ghost, with her pale face and white school nightgown. She had little Lottie tucked in front of her, and the child's gingery curls had been blown into a halo round her head. She was squealing and giggling with excitement, and actually *bouncing*, as though the dragon flight was an amazing treat, like a fairground ride.

Behind them, the other children clung to each other as the dragon hurled them through the air.

His smaller companions darted and twirled around them, and the silver dragon ignored their antics, only snorting occasionally as one of the other dragons shot across in front of his nose. Lily kept an eye out for the midnight creature who had rescued Peter, and was now carrying him caught up in its front claws. Peter swung and shifted as the dragon swooped, and Lily longed to scream to it to be careful. But she didn't dare. She'd never spoken to any of the other dragons, only seen them here and there in strange visions at Fell Hall. What if they weren't as helpful as the silver one? The black dragon had gleaming ruby eyes, and a mischievous look. It might drop Peter for the fun of catching him again.

At last the silver dragon slowed his wings, and spiralled gently down towards a patch of woodland below them. Lily watched the trees grow from something like a clump of dark green moss, taller and taller, until they swooped in amongst them, the dragon drawing in his wings, and landing in the fallen leaves with a gentle scrunch.

The children looked about them warily, reluctant to loosen their grip on the spiky frill that ran down the dragon's spine.

The dragon turned his head, peering back over his

shoulder. 'It's safe now, my dears,' he purred, his voice as low and gentle as he could make it. 'We'll rest here until dark, and then fly on to London tonight.'

'London,' some of the children whispered to each other, in a sort of delighted fear.

'We've a safe place to go,' Lily promised, crossing her fingers under a fold of her nightgown. She wasn't sure how Daniel and the other performers in the theatre were going to react to forty children. And a dozen dragons…

The other dragons were landing now, shooting in among the trees, and furling their wings gratefully. The blue-black dragon came down in an awkward fashion, with one front leg curled to his chest, and Peter pressed against his scales as saggy as a doll. He limped over to Lily, who was still perched on the silver dragon's back, and reared up, laying Peter down in front of her. The mute boy sprawled over the dragon's neck, staring up at Lily in bewilderment.

'Is he any better?' Georgie asked, leaning forward.

Lily sighed. 'Maybe a little. He's awake, anyway.' She bowed her head to the black dragon. 'Thank you – you were so clever to catch him; I thought he was lost for certain.'

The smaller dragon ducked his head smugly, and sidled away looking pleased with himself, to squabble over the best sleeping places with the others.

'He doesn't talk, like you?' Lily asked the silver dragon, curiously.

'Perhaps when we've been awake for longer... We've forgotten so much...' The dragon's voice was wistful. 'I learned again, from watching the children, and talking with you and your little dog.'

The little dog shook her ears irritably, but didn't argue for once. Flying had not agreed with Henrietta, and her black eyes were bulging even more than usual. She wriggled out from under Lily's arm and picked her way carefully towards Peter, until she stood over him, scowling thoughtfully.

'I'd hoped he would come back to himself, once he was away from Fell Hall. But he still seems to be bound up in those spells.' She sounded very grumpy, but Lily was sure that was nothing to do with Peter.

Lily stroked Henrietta gently, running her fingers along her velvety wrinkles, and the little dog nudged her hand. 'Will you be all right, all the way to London?' Lily murmured, hoping the dragon couldn't hear her. She didn't want to sound ungrateful.

Henrietta shuddered delicately. 'It may be better in the dark. When I can't see how far down everything is. Flying is unnatural.'

Henrietta said it quite clearly, and if the silver dragon hadn't been so big, and so noble-looking, Lily would have said that the noise he made was a snigger.

The children from Fell Hall were gradually loosening their frantic, panicked grip on the dragon's scales now, and sliding down his sides to the ground. Several of them staggered as their feet hit the dry leaves underfoot, their balance thrown by the hours in the air.

Georgie wriggled down, loosening her clutch on Lottie, who ran off, dancing round the trees and peeping out at the other dragons.

'Be careful!' Lottie's older sister, Elizabeth, hissed. 'Lottie, don't – don't annoy them,' she added in a fierce whisper, glancing nervously at the silver dragon as she hurried to follow Lottie.

'What do dragons eat?' Henrietta asked conversationally, leaning over the silver dragon's spiky crest and trying to see into his eyes.

The dragon stretched, and folded his wings more carefully, as though he was settling down for a while. 'Anything. All sorts of things… But not children, not now at least. I promise, and they do too.'

The other dragons twitched, and some of them looked quite regretful. The blue-black one pulled back in a clawed foreleg that had been creeping towards Lottie and sighed, sending out a misty plume of smoke that made the dry leaves dance and sizzle.

'You *can* breathe fire then,' Henrietta muttered,

shifting her paws a little nervously. 'Didn't like to ask. Well, it's useful, I suppose.'

'Perhaps we could have a campfire,' Georgie said hopefully. 'It was cold, flying. And we've only got our nightclothes on.'

Lily shook her head. 'What if someone saw the smoke?' She glanced around the wood, suddenly realising that it wasn't very big, and was extremely full of dragons. Tails were stretching out between the trees, and she was quite sure they'd flown over a village not far away. A village full of people who were probably awake, and maybe even setting out to gather firewood, or hunt rabbits, or just walk through the woods on their way somewhere. 'We need to hide,' she said anxiously to Georgie and Henrietta and the dragon. 'I hadn't thought!'

The dragon turned his head rather wearily. 'Can we hide here or must we fly on and find somewhere else? I can hardly fit behind a tree… And there are all the others too.'

Lily looked at him closely, hearing the cracks in his deep, velvety growl of a voice. He hadn't flown for hundreds of years, she realised. He hadn't done *anything* for hundreds of years. All the dragons had been sleeping for centuries, deep in the limestone caves under Fell Hall, until the growing tide of fallow magic in the country had woken them again.

She shook her head, and let herself slip down his side so that she could stand in front of him and look into his eyes. A dry membrane kept slipping over them as they talked, and she was sure his scales were dimmer. He had worn himself out rescuing them all.

'No, we'll stay here. None of us wants to move.' Several of the smaller dragons had curled themselves up like cats now, with their tails wrapped round their paws. She could even hear them purring. The children were huddled in little piles, leaning up against the tree trunks, or against dragon backs. They were casting anxious glances around – as though they still thought Miss Merganser and the others might be coming after them.

Lily reached up to lift Henrietta down, and held out a hand for the princess, who was wrapped round in layers of petticoats and a dress that had been grand, once. Then she looked hopefully at Georgie, who was shivering in her skimpy cotton nightgown, staring out between the trees. 'We can hide everybody... Don't you think? Couldn't we do a spell?'

Georgie shuddered. It was cold in the early-morning gloom of the wood, but Lily knew it was the thought of using her magic that chilled her, not only the wind. 'We could try,' Georgie muttered. 'But the spells are still inside me, Lily. The dragon unwound all that choking magic from Fell Hall, but the spells Mama planted haven't gone. I can feel them. They're awfully keen to be used. If I try any magic of my own, I'm scared they'll slip out too.'

Lily nodded, sighing. Georgie was probably right to be cautious. Their mother had been training her in magic, before they'd run away from their old home. She had filled Georgie with strange, dark spells, ones that the girls didn't understand, and that Georgie couldn't control.

'I think they're getting stronger,' Georgie murmured. She sounded guilty. She knew Henrietta thought she was weak, not being able to control the magic inside her.

In her worst moments, Lily agreed with the little black pug. She sometimes wondered if when she'd brought Henrietta out of that painting in their old house with her first real magic, she'd put the rudest, grumpiest bits of herself into the dog.

'As though they know it's almost their time...' Georgie rubbed her hands up and down her arms anxiously.

'We've got Princess Jane with us now,' Lily reminded her sister, trying to sound confident. 'She'll show us how to break into Archgate, and rescue Father.' She smiled at the little old lady, who was seated decorously on one of the dragon's forelegs. The princess glanced up from the little basket on her lap, and Lily bit her lip to stop herself smiling. Who else but a princess would carry on with their embroidery when sitting on a dragon in the middle of a damp and misty wood?

'I shall certainly do my best, my dears.'

'He'll know how to get rid of Mama's spells, Georgie. He must do.' Lily nodded firmly. She was trying to convince herself as much as Georgie. What if their father couldn't rescue her? Or wouldn't?

The girls hadn't seen him since Lily was tiny, since he'd refused to give up his magic, as every magician had been obliged to by the Queen's Decree. Lily had read a couple of his letters to her mother, but that was all she knew of him. That he sounded pleasant, and weary, and that he would rather be shut away in a magicians' prison than deny his birthright. They didn't know whether he had ever supported their mother in her plot against the queen. Maybe he wouldn't want to help them undo those strange spells. He might even send them straight back to Mama, so that she could keep working on Georgie. Lily bit her lip. They couldn't know – but at the same time, they had to do something, before the buried spells dug their claws deeper into Georgie.

'Use the rest of them,' Henrietta muttered, as she padded happily around the tree roots, sneezing and snuffling. She always said she was really a town dog, and preferred paving slabs under her paws, but she enjoyed the occasional country walk. Especially if it was followed by afternoon tea, with hot buttered toast.

Lily gazed blankly at her curly tail, bobbing about in the leaves, and Henrietta turned round, looking irritated. 'The others, Lily! Forty little magician children: use them! Well – say twenty, bearing in mind that half of them don't feel to me as if they've got a smidgen of magic blood. They probably just looked wrong, and some idiot packed them off to Fell Hall to be cleansed of a magic taint that wasn't there in the first place.'

Georgie stared at the other children, camped wearily around the little clearing. 'I never thought of that…'

Henrietta sniffed meaningfully, but didn't say anything. She was trying hard to be nicer to Georgie, but she slipped occasionally.

'It's a very good idea.' Lily nodded. 'Although… None of them has ever been trained in magic.'

'Neither have you!' Henrietta snapped back. 'It comes naturally, to those who have it. Let them try. The worst that happens is a tree falls on our heads.'

Lily swallowed, and looked around at the children from Fell Hall. They seemed to be recovering from their sudden dragonflight now. Some of the boys were pelting each other with dry leaves, and Lottie was still dancing about all over the place.

The dragon coughed solemnly, and the boys froze, as though they thought he might be about to crisp them with a blast of flame. 'The young lady wishes to speak to you.'

Lily felt suddenly tongue-tied. This was far more frightening than performing to an audience at the theatre. There she only had to scamper about, smiling foolishly, and be shut into cabinets. No one was expecting her to come up with a plan. The others gathered closer, and even the dozing dragons flickered their eyes open, in case she was going to say anything interesting.

'Um, we need to hide, in case anyone from the village sees us.'

'Will they be chasing us? From Fell Hall?' Elizabeth pulled Lottie close to her worriedly.

Lily shook her head. 'We've come quite a long way already. And last we saw of it, Fell Hall was collapsing, after the dragons came up out of the caverns. But we don't want to be seen anyway. We're still – well, outlaws, I suppose. And there aren't places to hide, here in the wood, so we'll have to do it by magic.'

Everyone stared back at her.

'What, a spell?' one of the boys said doubtfully at last.

Lily nodded. 'Why not? Lottie managed a spell early this morning.'

Lottie nodded importantly. 'Little birds flew round me! It was lovely. I want to do a spell, Lily!'

Lily looked around hopefully at the rest of the children. 'Does it feel like you shouldn't?'

While the children had been shut up at Fell Hall, the staff had fed them old, half-dead spells, designed to keep their own magic squashed deep down. Everyone had been taught that magic was wrong and shameful. When Lily and Georgie had first been taken there, they'd hoped to find other children like themselves, but instead the pupils had been bewitched into hating their own magical blood.

The boy wrinkled his nose and flexed his fingers. His feet twitched, and then he looked up at Lily, smiling hopefully. 'Actually, I'd like to,' he admitted. 'I never understood what they'd been doing to us. It feels like we've been set free. Not just from that place. Inside me as well, somehow.'

Mary raised a hand shyly. She was one of the children who'd been abandoned at Fell Hall as a baby, put into a strange stone cradle in the wall and left, because someone thought she was a witch baby.

'I don't feel that much different,' she said, sounding sorry. 'Less, um, misty. But I don't think I could do a spell. I never did think I could.'

Henrietta padded over to her and rubbed her soft,

wrinkly face against Mary's bare leg. 'I don't think you've got any magic in you,' she told Mary regretfully. 'Do you mind very much?'

Mary swallowed in a gulp, and sat down on the twig-scattered earth next to the dog. 'Not all that much… But what do I do now?'

Lily crouched next to her. 'None of us knows what we're going to do. The dragon says he'll carry us to the theatre, but after that – we don't know. But it's better to be anywhere else than at Fell Hall, isn't it?'

'You won't leave me behind because I can't do it?' Mary whispered.

The dragon snorted furiously, and Mary shrank back against Lily, trembling.

'I didn't mean to frighten you, dear one. I am angry, but not with you.' His tail thrashed from side to side among the trees, shaking leaves down on their heads. 'How has everything gone so wrong, since we slept?' He lowered his massive head towards Lily and Mary. 'You will *never* be left behind.' Then he drew himself up, curling his forelegs protectively around Princess Jane and nudging Peter, who was huddled on his back still. 'Those of you who feel you do not have the magic in you, come and sit with me.' The growl had softened back to a velvety purr. 'We shall watch. Delicious magic; it will be a treat.'

About fifteen of the children hurriedly separated themselves from the rest, mostly looking relieved. The dragon purred at them in welcome, wrapping his tail around his forelegs like a bench, and murmuring, 'Sit, dear ones. Sit.'

'Are we going to make a spell now? A proper spell?' Lottie asked eagerly, dancing up and down and pulling on Lily's arm. 'Please tell me how!'

'I don't really know how,' Lily said, glancing anxiously at Georgie and Henrietta. 'It just happens. Um. I suppose if we're doing a spell together, we all ought to think about the same things.'

'Hold hands,' Henrietta pointed out, scurrying busily around between their feet.

'Oh! Yes.' Lily caught Lottie's fat little hand, and held out her other hand to one of the boys, who took it rather gingerly. The boys and girls had been separated at Fell Hall, and he probably hadn't held a girl's hand in years. His hand was dry, and hot, and it was shaking.

'We need to hide ourselves,' Lily murmured, looking around at the nervous, excited faces. They were all gathered in a circle now, with Henrietta still weaving herself in and out as though she were playing some strange party game. Lily could feel more than just Lottie eagerly squeezing her fingers, and the shy boy's tentative grasp. Magic was humming round the circle already.

Years of pent-up power were sparking from fingertip to fingertip, and the boy holding her hand gasped excitedly as a sheen of silver washed itself over his arms.

'What's happening?' he whispered to her. 'I didn't do anything; I thought we'd have to say some words.'

'Sometimes you do,' Lily whispered back. 'But sometimes things happen without you really knowing why.' Henrietta nudged her leg, and peered up at her smugly. The glistening magic was coating her dark fur too.

'Think about hiding,' Lily said, raising her voice to speak to all of them.

All around the circle, children were gripping hands more tightly, half frightened, half gleeful, as their magic shone and sparkled among them. Lily saw that Lottie's gingery curls were glittering, as magic shone along every strand of hair. Elizabeth, her sister, squeaked as her own red hair unbound itself from its tight plait, twisting and swirling and growing almost to her toes.

'Hiding,' Lily said again, almost hating to call everyone back from this first joy of magic rushing through them. 'We have to be safe. Think of a wall that closes us in.'

'No!' the boy next to her hissed, almost pulling his hand away. 'Not after Fell Hall! No more walls.'

Lily nodded. 'A hedge then!' Magical stories had

grown unpopular since the queen had banished magicians, but she'd had an ancient book of fairytales at home in Merrythought House. She remembered a rose hedge, thorny and impenetrable. 'We'll make the trees seem thicker, and darker, and if people come past, they'll want to go round the wood, instead of through it.' She closed her eyes, thinking of vines and ivy and roses trailing in between the outer trees as a flowery barrier.

'Look…' Georgie whispered, and Lily's eyes flickered open again.

Elizabeth's red hair was twined with vines and tiny white wild roses, their thorny stems winding in and out. Her always worried, greenish eyes were sparkling now, and her grey-pale cheeks were pink. And beyond the trees a shadowy fence of flowers and leaves had grown up, not quite there…but Lily was fairly certain that anyone who tried to walk through it would find it was very real indeed.

'Oh…that was so exciting…' Elizabeth breathed, as the others broke out of the spell and stared at her.

'You've got a proper dress on,' one of the girls said admiringly. 'Look, she was in her nightgown before!'

It was true that Elizabeth was now wearing a long, trailing white dress, with sprays of silken flowers embroidered up and down the skirt.

'It's beautiful,' Georgie murmured, stroking it. 'Look at the stitching! That spell must have seen it inside you somehow. I'd never thought of doing embroidery by magic.'

Lily rolled her eyes at Henrietta. Georgie loved clothes, and would have liked nothing better than to work in the wardrobe at the theatre they'd lived in, making costumes for the ballet dancers. Lily couldn't think why anyone would sew for pleasure, and Georgie seethed about her little sister's torn, stained dresses. Magical embroidery didn't sound much more exciting than the normal kind to Lily.

Elizabeth and Georgie settled down by the princess, admiring the delicacy of the dress, and the others sat in groups, stretching out their fingers and trying to recapture that strange silver glow.

'That was lovely,' Lottie told Lily, yawning hugely, as they leaned against the dragon's warm scales. 'Can we do it again?' She was almost asleep.

'Later,' Lily promised. 'We ought to rest now – we have to fly again tonight.' But Lottie was asleep already.

It was half-dark by the time Lily woke, her arms prickly and aching from holding Lottie. Georgie was leaning against her, and Henrietta was curled up on her feet. Lily had a sudden, panicked moment, sure that she had lost someone, but still too wrapped up in her uncomfortable daytime sleep to work out who.

Then she saw that Peter was sitting up, his legs stretched out in front of him, against the dragon's neck. He still looked dazed but his eyes were open, wide open, and he was gazing at her, as though at last he had remembered who she was.

She smiled at him, hopefully, and he smiled slowly back, as though he was having to try hard to remember how to do it.

Lottie woke up, frowning, and patted Lily's hand. It was only a gentle little movement, but it was insistent, and as Lily turned back to look at the small girl, she realised that Lottie thought of her as the person in charge. The person who was going to make everything right.

'I'm hungry,' she told Lily, her voice wavering a little.

Lily nodded. 'I know. I am too, Lottie. But we don't have anything. It's hard to make food with magic – magic and nothing else, I mean. You need ingredients to start with.' She looked over at the dragon, who was stirring slowly, his wings rustling as he woke. 'We're going to fly to London,' she explained to Lottie. 'There'll be food at the theatre – or, at least, there's lots of places we can go and get some.'

Lottie wrinkled her nose, and seemed to be thinking about complaining. But even though she was only six, she could see quite well that there wasn't any food to whinge for.

The dragon yawned, and almost everybody huddling around him in the wood flinched. His teeth were very large and shiny when one had a close-up view of them like that. He closed his jaws with a satisfied snap, and gazed down at Lily. 'Shall we fly on?'

Lily nodded, and looked around for the other dragons, blinking as she tried to see them stretched out among the trees.

'They've gone,' the silver dragon told her with a smoky sigh.

Lily swallowed, imagining the playful troupe of dragons loose in the countryside. 'Where?'

He shook his wings a little, his eyes glittering in the dusk. 'I don't know where they'll go. But they will be careful. I explained. They found it very hard to understand that magic is no longer welcome, but they will stay hidden.'

'They won't hunt people, will they?' Lily whispered to him, rather anxiously.

The dragon rustled his wings again, and answered in a low, murmuring growl. 'I hope not. But then, they are wild…' He nudged her very delicately with the side of his huge face. The scales were surprisingly silky. 'They might eat people. But only people they don't like.'

Lily wasn't entirely sure if he was serious. Did

dragons tease? She was sure she'd read about them loving riddles, but that was all.

'You need to take off the spell,' he murmured to her, and she nodded. She'd almost forgotten. The little grove would have been abandoned for ever.

'I think the red-haired one needs to do it,' Henrietta said, nodding towards Elizabeth, who was smoothing the skirts of her new dress with a pleased expression. She looked up anxiously as she heard Henrietta.

'How do I?' Then her face fell a little. 'Do you think I'll have to give the dress back?' she asked sadly.

Lily nibbled her bottom lip. 'No… Why don't you try pulling out a hair? The spell made your hair grow, and you've still got flowers in it.'

Wincing a little, Elizabeth did as she was told, plucking one long, golden-red hair that twisted around her fingers as though it was still alive. 'Now what should I do?' she asked, gazing at it, and Lily thought furiously. She'd hoped that just pulling out the hair would do something to the spell, at least.

The dragon spat out a little flicker of flame, and the children gathered in between his forelegs scattered with yelps.

'Apologies,' he murmured. 'I forgot myself… Hold it here, young lady in the dress.'

Elizabeth held the hair out to him at arm's length,

worriedly eyeing his fiery mouth. The hair curled and coiled, and the dragon shot out one tiny flame that frizzled it to a twisted rope of ash which collapsed and blew away on the wind.

All at once the wood seemed lighter, the faint shadowy hedge around the trees melted away, and Lily could hear voices in the distance.

'We should go. It's dark enough, isn't it, if we keep high?'

The dragon nodded, and the children began to climb on again, settling themselves along the ridges of his spine. With his wings pressed close to his sides, he wormed his way between the trees to the open field beyond.

Lily felt Princess Jane's thin arms tightening around her waist as the wings stretched and beat, and they were up, in a rush of cold air and sharp-smelling magic.

TWO

'Look at the lights…' Lily murmured, as they circled slowly above the city. 'Don't forget to hold on,' she added sharply, listening to the gasps and sighs of admiration from behind her. All the children were leaning over the dragon's sides, peering down at the sparkling ribbons of light that tracked the streets of London.

'This city is a great deal larger than it used to be,' the dragon said thoughtfully. 'I suppose it's only to be expected.' But he sounded sad again, as though he was realising how much time he'd lost.

Lily ran a comforting hand over the back of his head – where his ears would be, except that she wasn't sure which of the scaly fronds actually were his ears. But he seemed pleased. She could feel his purring growl beneath her.

'Lily, how do we find the theatre from up here?' Georgie asked. Lily could hear that she was frowning.

'We can't. We'll have to go lower, so we can see the streets properly. It's close to the river, we know that...' But the river looked awfully long, even from up here. It wound through the city like a glistening snake.

'What if someone sees us?' one of the boys called, and Lily sighed.

'We haven't a choice. And I don't think anyone who saw us would believe what they were seeing anyway,' she added. 'No one thinks dragons exist any more, or that they ever did. Everyone knows they're only a story. If you saw a story flying over your house, you'd probably just go and hide your head under your pillow. I hope.'

The dragon chuckled. 'I think it would be a good thing if we were seen, Lily. We need to bring the magic back. What better way to start?'

Lily shivered. 'Not yet. We aren't ready.'

The dragon was silent for a moment. There wasn't even the slap of his wings against the wind, now that he was gliding down towards the glittering streets. 'Will you ever be ready?' he asked her at last.

Lily stared at the lights blurring and flashing beneath them and sighed. 'Maybe not. That's what you mean, isn't it? That we couldn't be ready for something like this. So we shouldn't worry if we aren't?'

'Indeed. I do not suggest that we are reckless. But you should be daring.'

'I don't feel daring,' Lily whispered, the words whipping away in the wind. 'I wish we could just stop, and have a rest for a while.' That was why she wanted so much to go back to the theatre, she realised. For a few short weeks, she and Georgie and Henrietta had lived there as though they might have stayed for ever. As though they weren't running away from their mother and her strange plots. And as though all they knew of magic were the illusions they assisted with on stage.

Then the dragon shivered underneath her with one of those strange purring growls, and Henrietta darted her head down to lick Lily's arm, and Lily shook herself. She was flying over London on the back of a dragon. Until a few weeks before, she'd thought that her family's magical blood had missed her out, and she'd never imagined anything as amazing as this.

She wondered how many magicians there were, hidden away around the country, burying their magic deep inside themselves. They'd never know what it was like to fly on a dragon, or even join hands and surround themselves with magic as she and the others had done, back in the wood.

'Perhaps just a little bit daring,' she said to the dragon. 'We don't want the Queen's Men searching for us.'

He nodded. 'I think those that have magic inside them may be looking, Lily. I can feel them, wishing, as I fly...'

'There must be hundreds.' Lily caught her breath excitedly as he swooped down lower, gliding past the attic windows of the tall houses, and arcing out over the river. She could hear Georgie and Lottie behind her, Lottie squealing delightedly as they skimmed across the water, and Georgie telling her not to wriggle so much.

'The theatre isn't far from that bridge, Lily!' Georgie yelled. 'We walked across it once, remember? Tell him to turn in line with the bridge, and fly south. I think, anyway...'

'I heard her,' the dragon told Lily, banking to the right and dipping over the ornate metal bridge. He must have looked like some strange cloud, or a wisp of mist off the river. Only a pair of horses drawing a delivery van spooked at the sight of him, rearing and twisting against the shafts of the wagon. Lily could hear their driver cursing.

'So horses don't like dragons, then?' she asked him, and he snorted.

'Nothing on four legs likes us, dear one. They know

we'd happily eat them.' He chuckled. 'Your little dog pretends that she understands no such thing, but she's not very convincing. Ah, is this it? All lit up? I can hear music.'

'Yes!' Lily shrieked delightedly, ignoring the furious muttering from Henrietta. 'Do you think you could land in that yard at the back? Is it big enough?'

The dragon circled lower, and eyed the yard thoughtfully. 'If I land there, Lily, it will be difficult for me to take off again. I could do it, but it would be slow; I'd have to claw my way up. Are you sure we're safe here?'

Lily gulped, and turned back to Georgie, who nodded. 'It's the safest place there is.' She had her fingers crossed behind Lottie's back, Lily could tell.

'Not that that means much,' Henrietta muttered crossly.

'Land,' Lily told him. 'If – if something goes wrong –' she didn't want to think what – 'then we'll make some sort of spell. We won't let anyone hurt you.'

He snorted kindly. 'I am more worried that someone will injure *you* fragile little things. Dragons are hard to hurt.'

The little yard at the back of the theatre led onto the scene dock, where the huge canvas flats were painted. A gate led out of the yard into the rabbit warren of alleys that crisscrossed the grander streets around the theatre.

The dragon settled into a tighter spiral, corkscrewing down towards the cobbles, and eventually slipped into the tiny yard with a rustle of enormous wings. There was very little space left.

'And now we wait?' he asked. 'I can hear music still. Is there a play, now?' His eyes were glinting eagerly, and Lily rubbed soothing fingers across his scales.

'A show, yes, it must be nearly the end.'

'That's Daniel's music,' Georgie said quietly, smiling a little. 'I can tell. It's the floating girl trick. He's found someone to replace us, Lily.'

'Well, that's good, isn't it…' Lily tried to sound as though she didn't mind – they'd left the theatre, after all. It must have been about ten days ago, she thought, trying to count back in her head. 'We told him to. We went off with Aunt Clara, remember. To see if she could tell us where Father was.'

Their mother's sister had been in the audience, and she had searched the girls out the next day. Lady Clara Fishe had hidden her magic so well, and for so long, that even she didn't realise she was still using glamours to keep up appearances as a society lady. She had been horrified that Lily and Georgie might let the family's dirty little secret out, and put her son, the girls' cousin Louis, in danger. When they'd been denounced as magicians, she had hurriedly washed her hands of them, and seen them sent away to Fell Hall.

'Still… I'd thought we might be able to go back into the act,' Georgie sighed.

Lily frowned at her. 'The Queen's Men, Georgie, remember? We've already been seized once, and now we've escaped! We're in hiding, we can't go prancing about on stage!'

'I suppose so…'

'Dim-witted,' Henrietta pronounced with relish, in a carrying whisper. 'Feather-brained as they come.'

Lily shook her head and murmured back, 'She's only wishing, Henrietta. I wish we could, too.'

A storm of applause swelled out from the theatre, and Lottie and several of the smaller children woke up in fright, clutching at the others.

'Just a few more minutes,' Lily promised. 'We need to let the audience leave. And then we'll tell them that we're here.'

'And we can have supper,' Lottie remembered, sleepily pleased.

Lily nodded. The Queen's Theatre had a delicate little gold-painted supper room, where ices were sold, but it was not used to catering for forty hungry children. Still, that was hardly worth worrying about. She had to explain away a dragon first. She slipped down from the dragon's neck, holding up her arms to Henrietta. The little pug dog had been the petted darling of the theatre crew. Now she darted happily back through the peeling double doors, sniffing enthusiastically at the strange, dusty theatre smell, and searching for the stagehands who had fussed over her with scraps.

'Hey, Sam, look!' A voice came from deeper within the passageways. 'It's the little dog back. Here, sweetheart, where did you spring from?'

Lily hurried round the corner after Henrietta, and found her sitting up on her hind legs, waving her front paws prettily at Sam, the head carpenter, who had made all of Daniel's amazing illusions, and his assistant Ned.

'Miss Lily! You're back!' Sam swung her up into his arms and kissed her cheek, scratching her with his bristly moustache. 'Did you not like it, with that grand aunt of yours? What are you doing here in your nightclothes? Ned, fetch her one of those drapes; she ain't decent, and she'll catch her death.' Sam flung a gaudy stage hanging around Lily's shoulders. 'She didn't throw you out on the street, did she, that sour-faced puss?'

Lily hugged him back. 'We got found out, Sam. Two other magician girls, they lived next door – they were jealous, and they betrayed us to the Queen's Men.'

Sam put her down in a hurry, holding her at arm's length and scanning her face anxiously. 'Those – those –'

He obviously couldn't think of a word to describe the queen's enforcers that he could say in front of Lily. 'Them! What did I tell you, Ned? Worse every day! Did they hurt you?'

'They took us to Fell Hall. Have you heard of it? It's a school for children with magic – they send the children there to try and squash the magic out of them. But we escaped.' Lily twisted her fingers together, looking up at Sam anxiously. He was very soft-hearted, she knew, and he had daughters of his own, although they were grown now. 'And we brought all the other children with us...' she added.

Ned stared at her. 'Here?'

Lily nodded. 'In the yard. About forty of them. And...'

Henrietta sniggered, but Ned had already raced off, calling back that he would fetch Daniel.

'Are you all right, Lily?' Sam was still holding her hands and looking at her as though he thought she might fall over. 'How did you get back here? Where is this Fell Hall? I've not heard of anywhere like that in London.'

Lily swallowed. She could hear Ned dashing back down the passageway, and others following. He'd probably told half the performers and the crew by now, he was such a blabbermouth. 'It's in Derbyshire...'

'How on earth did you get back here then?' Sam swung round to grab Daniel by the arm, as he hurried towards them. 'She's back! They had her and Miss Georgie shut up in some reform school up north, but the girls escaped, and they've got all the other children with them.'

Daniel looked particularly wild-eyed, half out of his Eastern magician costume, with his false rat-tail moustache hanging at an improbable angle. 'I thought you were safe with your aunt!' He sounded bewildered. 'No, explain later. We'd better bring these children in. You were right to come back here, Lily. Who knows what we'll do with them, but we'll manage somehow. Have you had anything to eat?'

Henrietta pawed his leg, her black eyes sparkling wickedly, and he bent down to pick her up. 'Hello – I wasn't ignoring you, I'm sorry. It's just rather a shock.'

'You haven't heard anything yet,' Henrietta murmured. The whole theatre had seen Lily use her magic, when she'd had to rescue one of the other performers from a metal bar that was falling out of the rigging. They'd kept the girls' secret, but it wasn't widely known that Henrietta could talk; she only spoke to Sam, who she adored, and to Daniel and a few of the other performers.

'How many of these children are there?' Daniel

asked, looking from Henrietta to Lily anxiously.

'There's forty, but that isn't what she means…' Lily swallowed. 'Daniel, when we escaped from Fell Hall, we had help. I found – I found someone in the house – two someones, actually,' she added remembering that she had to explain a princess as well. 'One of them helped us escape, and he brought us back here. He wants to stay; he thinks he likes theatres, although he hasn't seen a play for a very long time.' She stopped, not quite sure how to break the news.

'Just tell him!' Henrietta hissed.

'Look…' The dancers and the contortionists and the other acts were still gathering in the passageway as the news spread, all wrapped in dressing gowns, and patchy with stage make-up. One of the ballet dancers was pointing to the door out to the yard, where a little knot of weary-looking children had appeared, led by Georgie.

'Poor little mites…' Lily could hear everyone muttering sympathetically, and Sam hurried forward to pick up Lottie, who was almost asleep on her feet. But he stopped at the door, staring upwards.

'Mr Daniel, you'd better come here.' His voice was even gruffer than usual, as if he was having to force his words out past something stuck in his throat.

Henrietta leaped out of Daniel's arms and skittered towards the door, growling. She set herself in front of

Sam's feet, glaring up at the silvery dragon, who was peering curiously in through the doors. 'Don't you scare him!' she snapped. 'He's mine!'

The dragon had excellent manners, Lily thought gratefully, running after her and tripping on the gaudy drape she was wearing. Henrietta wouldn't even be a snack for a creature that size, but it didn't stop her being rude. The dragon merely drew his head back slightly, and bowed.

'Miss Lily…' Sam muttered. 'What have you brought us?'

'Is it an automaton?' Daniel asked, staring at her and blinking. 'I've never seen one so large, but I suppose it would be possible. Though how you got it in here, I can't see…'

'I flew,' the dragon told him helpfully. 'It was a rather complicated landing, and I have to tell you, it may be difficult for me to get out again.'

'A talking automaton.' Daniel swallowed. It was easier for him to believe that the dragon was some sort of machine, Lily could see. He couldn't quite bring himself to accept that there was a real dragon sitting outside his theatre. He'd studied the history of magic, to create his illusionist's act, and he loved it. Lily was sure he secretly wished he could do real magic too. But this was something else.

'That's no automaton,' Sam muttered. 'Look at it. You couldn't make that. I couldn't, even… And it can fly?' He rounded on Lily, his eyes eager. 'It really flies?'

'All the way from Derbyshire.' Lily nodded.

Sam let out an ecstatic sigh. He slipped through the crowd of children and walked slowly out into the yard, gazing admiringly up at the dragon's scaly bulk. 'A wonder. That's what it is. A wonder.'

The dragon watched him, amused, but flattered too, Lily could tell. Back at Fell Hall, she and Henrietta had once persuaded him into appearing by telling him how amazing he was.

'Can I see?' Sam asked eagerly, reaching out a shaking hand towards one of the silvery wings.

The dragon obligingly stretched it out as far as he could in the tiny yard, and there was a hiss of disbelief from the theatre people gathered in the doorway.

Sam whistled through his teeth and then shook his head suddenly. 'Forgot myself. I'm sorry. Better get you inside, all these little ones, and you too, sir, if you'll fit. Reckon we can get him in through the scene dock if we open the doors, Mr Daniel?'

Daniel nodded. He still had a rather blank expression on his face, but he directed some of the other stagehands to open the huge doors. Sam lifted down the last of the children from the dragon's back, and beckoned him to follow.

The dragon wriggled delicately through the doors, twisting himself this way and that until he was coiled neatly in the cavernous space behind the stage. Forty children huddled next to him, staring anxiously at Lily's friends from the theatre. Some of them had been abandoned at Fell Hall as babies, and even the youngest of them had been at the school for years. They were used to being told that they were evil, and infected with magic. They didn't expect to be welcomed.

Maria, the wardrobe mistress who had taught Georgie to sew, came hurrying forward, her arms laden with a strange assortment of garments. 'There isn't much that's the right sizes,' she muttered. 'But they'll need more than those nightclothes. Oh, hurry up, girl, do!' she called crossly to the dancer behind her, who was carrying more clothes but obviously didn't want to come any closer to the dragon.

Georgie took the bundle from the frightened girl, trying to smile encouragingly, and started to pick out clothes and wrap the younger children in them.

'Are there more – more dragons?' Daniel murmured to Lily.

'Yes. But they went back. They helped us escape, but they wanted to live wild.'

'This one likes theatres?' Daniel remembered.

'He's lived at Fell Hall for hundreds of years. I think they had travelling players,' Lily explained.

'Can he keep still?' one of the scenery painters called to her suddenly.

The dragon swung his huge head round, and stared at the man, who swallowed nervously. 'I only meant – sir – that you'd make a fine backdrop for some of the acts. It would be something grand to have you on stage. All that fuss they made, at the Pavilion Theatre, about their stage waterfall. We'd have them beat.'

'I can keep still,' the dragon agreed. 'I could watch the play?'

'Hang on, hang on. They're staying?' someone muttered from the back of the crowd. 'Load of escaped children, and a dragon? What about the Queen's Men?'

'Would you throw them out into the street?' Maria snapped, turning round from trying to persuade Nicholas, one of the orphans, into a pair of pink silk trousers that he wasn't at all convinced about.

'It's a fire risk,' one of the contortionists pointed out.

'I could be,' the dragon agreed. 'But I would endeavour not to be.'

'Accidents happen,' the contortionist said gloomily.

'We have plenty of space,' Daniel said slowly. 'There are rooms where the children can sleep, enough space for the dragon, even. But if word gets out to the Queen's Men…' He turned to Lily, frowning. 'They're getting more vicious by the day. Queen Sophia has been ill, did you hear? Very ill. Last week her mother was confirmed as Queen Regent, by an Act of Parliament. And she is the one who cannot stand magicians. Far more so than her daughter. The Queen's Men are out patrolling the streets now, on the watch for any hint of something unlawful. They *want* to find it – they're taking people away for no reason at all.'

'It's horrible…' A beautiful, dark-eyed woman had come to help Maria, and now she stroked Elizabeth's fall of red hair, shaking her head. 'Who knows what they would do with you all if they caught you, Lily. I've booked a passage to America, now, you know. I have friends in New York, and I can work there as well as here. I shall work my way over, too; I've been booked to sing on board the ship.'

Lily nodded. Colette had an amazing singing voice; she made the theatre's chandeliers ring with her high notes, and she was kind as well. She'd shown Lily and Georgie how to put on their greasepaint without making themselves look like clowns.

'I'm not the only one. London's changing. I don't know what it's like in the other cities, but I can't stay, it frightens me.' She tweaked the gauzy skirt she'd pinned up round Lottie, and laughed, rather sadly. 'I'll miss it here.'

'We'll miss you.' Daniel sighed. 'I wish you'd change your mind, Colette. We're getting a full house every night now. You'll have to build your reputation all over again in New York.' Colette still shook her head, and Lily stared at Daniel in surprise. 'You're full every night? It was only Saturdays, before.'

'It's the illusions,' Sam told her proudly. 'Real popular, they are. Been a lot of talk about them in the papers, the last couple of weeks.'

Daniel smiled, and stared shyly at his boots. 'People still can't decide if they're real, you see. Even though I've explained to all these journalists that we've been investigated by the Queen's Men, and it's all trickery, only fake magic, they still want to believe. The audiences are fascinated.' He looked up at Lily suddenly. 'People are starting to want it back, Lily.'

'And so they should,' the dragon rumbled. 'Life is nothing without a little magic to spice it up.'

Daniel nodded. He was starting to look more comfortable standing next to a dragon. Especially a dragon he agreed with. 'Well, I think so too. But no one wanted it here, not for years. And now more people are starting to think like us. The Queen's Men have never been really popular, but everyone used to think they were right to take away magicians. I saw a boy throw a stone at one of their carriages yesterday, and the people in the street actually cheered. An old lady in a huge black crinoline stood in front of the alley he ran down, pretending she was having trouble with her umbrella, so they couldn't chase him. She nearly had one of the officers' eyes out.'

Lily ran her hand along the dragon's scales, glancing up at him excitedly. He had been right. Perhaps it was the time, after all.

He nodded to her. 'I can feel it, shifting in the air. Bubbling up out of the ground, dear one. It needs using.'

'All that doesn't make it any safer for us to have a blasted dragon in the theatre! Let alone these magician brats. They'll probably betray us all with some spell gone wrong! They can't stay here.'

Lily stepped back against the dragon's side, her fingers pressed into the warm scales, as the man strode forward. It was Alf, one of the brothers who performed a comic double act. Lily had always found it strange that he spent his life on stage making people laugh, but as soon as the curtains closed, he was one of the most miserable, grumpy people she'd ever met. He was also very big, and he towered over her.

Of course, the dragon towered over him. Even Alf recoiled slightly as the enormous silvery-white head lowered towards him. But he planted his feet firmly, and glared back into the sparkling eyes. 'Who's with me?'

There was a ripple of uncertain muttering from the crowd, and Daniel took a step towards Alf, with Sam right behind him.

'This is my theatre—'

'Excuse me.' The voice was quiet, and sweet, but somehow carrying, and Lily caught her breath as Princess Jane stepped out of the shadows behind the scenery.

Daniel bowed. Princess Jane's dress was worn and old-fashioned, but there was something about her face that made it impossible not to be polite – even though he had no idea who she was. 'Lily, you didn't say you'd brought a lady with you too. Would you like a chair, Miss?'

'Thank you, but I shall be quite comfortable here.' The princess smiled at the dragon, and waved a hand at him. Instantly, he curled out one foreleg so that she could sit, arranging her skirts with delicate twitches until the faded fabric hung beautifully.

'She's ever so familiar-looking,' Maria muttered. 'Is she an actress, Lily?'

'You may be seeing the resemblance to my sister,' the princess told her, smiling slightly. 'I am afraid that if you are all too frightened to keep a dragon, you will not want me in your theatre either. The Queen's Men would be particularly interested to know where I am.'

Sam muttered something that made Daniel kick him, then turned scarlet, and swept off his cap. 'It's her!'

Daniel glared at him. 'Who?'

'Look at her! Put a crown on her! *Imagine her on a stamp!*'

Daniel swung back to stare at Princess Jane, and gasped, along with most of the rest of the crowd.

Colette swept a dramatic and perfect curtsey, and even Alf bowed.

'Miss – Ma'am – Highness…' Sam stuttered. 'You're dead! They gave out that you had a wasting sickness. There was a state funeral – they floated rose petals down the river off little boats. I've got a mug! Black and gilt, with your portrait!'

'How very imaginative of someone…' The princess smiled. 'I should have liked to have seen the rose petals. However, I should think I was already imprisoned at Fell Hall by then. They kept me in my rooms at the palace for a few months, while they tried to persuade me to denounce magic. That would been what they called the wasting sickness, I suppose.'

'She shut you up, all this time? But it's been forty years… Your own sister?' Maria whispered.

Princess Jane shook her head. 'I think not. My

mother, more likely. Sophia was much more soft-hearted. She may not have known. I hope not,' she added wistfully. Then she turned and stared at Alf, her faded blue eyes suddenly sharp. 'The dragon is under my protection, as are the children. I intend to help Lily and Georgiana rescue their father, and restore magic to its proper place in our country. My dear sister has been misled, and so have her people.'

Daniel gulped. 'Are you proposing to become queen yourself? Is this, er, a revolution?'

The princess's eyes widened. 'Of course not...' She paused. 'Well, I hadn't thought of it that way, at least. Oh dear. Perhaps it is.' The steely gleam in her eyes dulled, leaving her looking much older. But the dragon lowered his head towards her, rubbing his huge face against hers, and purring.

Lily could see the magic rising off him in a cloud of misty silver, sparkling faintly around the old princess's white hair, and sharpening her features so she looked almost young again, and strong. She sat up straighter. 'We will do whatever is needed,' she told Daniel and the others, sounding even more royal than she had before.

THREE

Lily stared anxiously up into the sky. It was September now, and the nights were growing colder. She shivered, wishing she still had some of the beautiful clothes that Aunt Clara had provided for her and Georgie, when they were still her pretty little nieces. They had all been left behind when the girls were sent to Fell Hall. Aunt Clara had probably burned them.

Georgie and Maria and the others had done the best they could from what was in the big wicker hampers in the theatre wardrobe, but there were forty children to clothe, and it was a case of one dress and feel lucky. Lily wrapped the piece of old velvet curtain she was using as a cloak more tightly round her shoulders.

'Can you see him yet?' Georgie slipped out of the doors and into the yard.

'No. Nothing. What if someone caught them?' Lily wrapped her arms round her chest tightly and blinked a few times, her eyes stinging. She'd been gazing up at the stars for too long. It was after midnight now – maybe even one or two in the morning.

'I don't see how they could,' Georgie said slowly. 'He'd just fly off, wouldn't he? No one would be able to stop him. Unless they had, I don't know, a cannon… It's just taking a long time.'

Henrietta nudged Lily's ankle comfortingly. 'There were a lot of places he had to get to, Lily. And most of those children couldn't give him very clear directions. They hadn't been home for years.'

'I suppose…' Lily blinked again, and shook her head wearily. Her eyes were starting play tricks on her – a patch of stars had just gone out. Which wasn't possible. She dropped the curtain, shielding her eyes with one hand and gazing up. 'It's him! Look, Georgie, that dark patch – it's him, it has to be!'

Georgie frowned upwards, and then grabbed Lily's arm and hauled her backwards into the shelter of the doorway. Henrietta came skittering after them as the dragon executed a showy spiral landing into the yard. He lowered his head towards them, his dark eyes sparkling with excitement. 'You were waiting for me, dear ones?'

'We were worried about you,' Lily admitted. 'It's been hours.'

'Some of the smaller villages were difficult to find,' the dragon admitted. 'We had to resort to dropping down and reading signposts; it was most undignified. And I fear at one point we may have disturbed a courting couple behind a haystack.'

'But you took them all back?' Lily asked eagerly.

'Every one.' He sounded most definitely smug, now.

Out of the forty children from Fell Hall, only Lily and Georgie, and Peter, Mary and Nicholas, all three of whom were orphans, were left at the theatre. The others had all gone back to their families. Many of them had lived in London – it had always been a city full of magicians – and they had gone quietly home after a night spent at the theatre. Lily had worried that some of them wouldn't be welcomed by their families, but so far none of them had come back, and yesterday they had received a grateful letter from one of the girls' parents, overjoyed at the safe return of their darling.

The dragon had agreed to return those who lived further away to their old homes, if they wished to go. Even though Daniel had promised that he'd find work at the theatre somehow, for anyone who wanted to stay, all the children with families had decided to go back home.

'I wonder if we'll ever see any of them again,' Lily murmured. 'I'll miss Lottie.'

'They'll come back to London when they're older. Elizabeth promised Maria she would. She's going to practise that embroidery spell, and work out more of them. Maria thinks she'll make a fortune as a dressmaker to the Quality.'

Lily sighed. 'But will she? What if their parents won't let them use their magic? What if they won't take them back? Elizabeth said her parents didn't write to her any more, do you remember? Hardly anyone ever got letters from home.'

The dragon curled himself wearily on the cool flagstones of the yard, and sighed. 'Then they'll come back here, Lily. I breathed magic into every one of those children before I left them, showing them how to find their way back. If they aren't welcomed into their old homes, the magic will bring them to me.' He glanced sideways at the door behind the girls, and murmured to Lily. 'The boy is here.'

Lily turned to see Peter standing in the open doorway. He was scribbling in the little scarlet-bound notebook that Daniel had given him, and Lily leaned over to see what he had written.

Did they all go?

She nodded, and looked at him, shaping her words as clearly as she could so that he could read her lips in the shadowy yard. 'Yes. All of them. It's only us and Mary and Nicholas now.'

I should go too. He wrote it slowly, his hands jerking uncontrollably. He still hadn't shaken off the lingering effects of the spells that had been used to drug him at Fell Hall, but now Lily could see the old Peter, deep inside. It was almost harder to watch him fighting inside this shell of a body that wouldn't do what he wanted, than it was to see him lifeless and doll-limp.

'You can't! Where would you go?' she demanded, glaring at him.

He shrugged, his shoulders twisting.

'He needs something to do.' The dragon had crawled closer to the doorway so he could stare at Peter, who was trying to stare back without looking scared. 'Doesn't he? Ask him; he can't understand me, for I don't speak in the same way you do.'

Lily looked back at Peter in surprise, and realised that the dragon was right. Peter had no idea what he'd said – the dragon had no lips to read.

'It isn't just charity, you know,' she said slowly. 'Sam could use your help. Especially if Daniel goes ahead with all these new illusions.'

Daniel had been using Elsie, one of the girls from the

ballet troupe, as his assistant since Lily and Georgie had gone, but she hated the job, even though she was paid more. She particularly detested the trick where she had to be sawn into pieces, as she was taller than Lily, and she was convinced every night that Daniel was going to cut her toes off. She'd begged Lily to take her old role back again, but the girls had decided it wasn't safe for them to be seen on stage. Lily was pretty sure that Aunt Clara had told the Queen's Men everything. She and Georgie had to stay hidden, in case they came to the theatre searching.

Henrietta was particularly disappointed. She had adored being a show-dog, and the audiences had loved her. She tried to persuade Daniel that she could be part of the act again if she was powdered. She wouldn't even mind people thinking she was a common or garden fawn pug, as she put it. But he didn't think it would be convincing enough, and Lily pointed out that Henrietta jumped around so much catching handkerchiefs and bunches of flowers that the powder would probably all fall off.

Lily had persuaded Daniel to try Nicholas and Mary in the act instead, as Elsie was so desperate to go back to being a dancer. The two orphans had been reluctant at first. Neither of them remembered any life outside Fell Hall, and they found the idea of an audience very strange. But Mary was even thinner and smaller than Lily, and she was won over by Daniel's extravagant praise when he saw how beautifully she fitted in all the cabinets. No one had ever said such encouraging things to her, and she was blossoming.

Nicholas was mostly persuaded by Maria, who promised to make him a whole outfit of everyday clothes in plain brown, instead of the hated pink silk trousers, if only he would try.

Having two assistants again had fired Daniel with a new enthusiasm for designing illusions. Mary had no magic of her own, but away from Fell Hall, Nicholas was finding that magic kept spilling out of him. He had to try very hard not to add real magic into the tricks, and kept complaining to Lily about how difficult it was.

'I can't not...' he muttered to her, when everyone had yelled at him for turning the white rabbit into a strange green furry creature that had nearly bitten Daniel's hand off when he tried to pull it out of the hat. 'I didn't mean to. I just thought about it, and it sort of happened.'

'You mustn't think about it,' Lily said sternly. 'What if it happens when there's an audience?' But then she'd spoilt it by giggling. Daniel's face had been so very funny. It had taken Lily a good half an hour to turn the rabbit back again, and she'd only managed it in the end by borrowing some of the dragon's strength. He had been curled up along the back of the stage, watching in fascination. Fake magic was something he had never come across before.

The dragon was right, she could see it now. Peter needed something to do, too. She'd been neglecting him, Lily realised guiltily, seeing at last how unhappy he looked. He was safe and fed and clothed, and she'd rescued him twice, and then she had stopped worrying about him. She was so happy to be back at the theatre that she had assumed everyone else was happy there too.

Before he had been taken to Fell Hall, Peter had been a servant boy at Merrythought, the house where Lily and Georgie's family had hidden themselves away after the Decree that had banned magic. Their father had been imprisoned, and their mother had sworn that she had given up all magic. It had been a strange, empty house, with only a few servants. No one had wanted to work there, and the villagers across the narrow strait had thought the place was cursed. Peter had been found abandoned on the beach – his family hadn't wanted him because he was a mute, everyone had assumed. After that, he had worked for his keep. He wasn't used to being idle.

'You could help Sam.' Lily nodded thoughtfully. 'You're good at mending things; you always did that back at the house.'

Peter stared at her and extended one hand, showing her how much it shook.

Lily sighed and ran her fingers lightly over the back of Peter's. His skin was greyish, his outdoor tan faded from being shut up inside at Fell Hall. 'The spells left you shaky,' she told him. 'I can feel them, the rags of the magic. But that'll go. It will, won't it?' she asked the dragon.

'Probably,' the dragon agreed.

Lily decided not to repeat the exact words. 'He says it'll get better,' she told Peter. 'Even if your hands are shaky, there are things you could do. And we might need your help too,' she added. 'Once Princess Jane is feeling stronger, she's going to tell us how to get into Archgate.'

Peter frowned, obviously not sure what she meant.

'I didn't know either. It's the magicians' prison. We were so close to it, all the time we were in London, but no one knew! There's a big white marble arch at the front of the palace, like a grand entrance. And the prison's inside it, or under it, I think – it wouldn't be big enough otherwise.'

You want to get in it? Peter's writing looped madly over the page.

'That's where Father is. We're almost sure. We have to get him out. He's the only person who knows Mama's magic well enough to take off the spells she laid inside Georgie.'

Georgie smiled at him sadly. 'I'm just as broken as you. Except I'm getting worse, not better.'

Peter stared at her, his eyes dark and serious. He'd never known her as well as he knew Lily – Georgie had been shut up with the girls' mother all the time they were at Merrythought, being taught the spells that had coiled themselves deep inside her, waiting to be released. Even Lily had been frightened of her some of the time then, she was so pale and ghost-like.

I thought you were staying here. Didn't know you had more to do. His sallow face flushed pinker, and he nodded determinedly. *I'll stay till you've found him then. You need someone to look after you.* He shut the book with a snap and stowed it in his pocket, then headed back down the passageway before Lily could argue with him. Not that she would have done, or not much at least. She could see that already there was a new determination in his step; the awful dragging look of him had gone.

Princess Jane had been given the largest and least shabby of the rooms under the theatre. Daniel had wanted to go out and buy some new furniture that was slightly more fitting for a princess than the battered old iron bedstead that was already there, but the others had persuaded him that it might arouse the suspicions of the Queen's Men. He had insisted that one of the scene painters should paint a coat of arms over the bed at least.

The princess had been exhausted by the journey, and her dramatic confrontation with Alf and the other theatre people. She had declared that she really didn't care what the bed looked like, as long as she could sleep in it. Since then she had been holding court, propped up on pillows, and wearing a purple marabou-trimmed cape that Maria felt was appropriate for royalty.

Lily slipped into her room the next morning, hoping that the princess would be awake. Now that all the other children had been sent home, she was anxious to find out more about Archgate. The passages under the stage were full of hurrying people – Daniel had decided that Mary and Nicholas and the new illusions were ready to be shown to the audience tonight, and since he had demanded a whole new set to be made, to show off the dragon to the best advantage, there was still a great deal of work to be done. Lily had asked Sam if Peter could help, and she had left him stubbornly polishing the new cabinets to a mirror-like shine.

Henrietta leaped up onto the patchwork quilt that Sam had brought from home – it had been his grandmother's, and had a faint, pleasant scent of lavender and old ladies.

Princess Jane was working on her delicate embroidery, and curled up on the quilt next to her was

Georgie, practising stitches on a piece of linen.

'What are you doing here?' Lily asked, almost accusingly.

'Just sewing.' Georgie sounded bewildered.

'We're supposed to be setting you free of these spells, not teaching you fancy stitches,' Lily told her. Then she bobbed her head apologetically at the princess. 'Sorry.'

'Sewing can be very settling to a troubled mind, Lily.' The princess tucked her work away in its little basket, and sighed. 'Your sister needs something to occupy her hands. She's frightened.'

Georgie stared down at her embroidery, her hair hanging over her face.

'I suppose…' Lily muttered. 'I came to ask about the prison, Your Highness.'

'I think while I am here, it would be better simply to call me Miss Jane, don't you? If we all get used to that, it will be safer when there are visitors.'

Lily nodded. 'Miss Jane. Do you still think you can get us inside Archgate?' she asked eagerly.

'If the spells haven't been changed,' the princess said thoughtfully. 'They know I escaped now, we must suppose. The warders of Fell Hall must have reported what happened. But I imagine they would expect me to try to escape abroad, to one of my other sisters, Lucasta or Charlotte.' She chuckled. 'Why would I be so foolish as to come to London?' She leaned back against the pillows, closing her eyes. 'It was a very long time ago, girls. But I went into the prison with my mother and Sophia. Only once. My mother wished to question a magician who was held there, to ask for information about my father's murderer. She wanted to go herself. She needed us.'

'Why?' Henrietta wriggled closer, resting her heavy dark chin on the princess's bony knees.

'She couldn't open the door herself. Only one of the royal blood, you see? Our mother had married into the royal line, she was not born to it.'

Lily frowned. 'What if you were all on holiday? Or ill? Surely the king or queen didn't have to open the door every time someone wanted to go in or out?'

'The warders had special keys, which they wore on chains around their necks. A tiny pinprick's worth of blood embedded in each one, and they would only work for that one person. Anyone else who wanted to enter needed one of us.'

'I see.' Lily was frowning. 'Is that all, though? When you visited before, did you only have to stand in front of the door, and it opened for you? It was that simple?'

Princess Jane shook her head. 'No. I would only be able to open the outer doors. After that we would have to use your magic to go further – there are locks, and spells, and strange guards on every passage.'

'What sort of guards?' Lily looked worriedly at Georgie.

'When the prison was first built, after the great war with Talis, when magicians were first starting to be feared, the greatest magicians of the day helped design its wards. Rose, the girl I told you about, she and her master, Aloysius Fountain, spent weeks sealing spells into the stones.'

'Our magic wouldn't be strong enough for that, Lily,' Georgie said anxiously. 'Even if I were to let Mama's spells out, I don't think we could do it.'

'We *are* strong,' Lily said doubtfully.

'Strong enough to wake a dragon, and free us all from Fell Hall,' the princess agreed.

'But you aren't trained. It isn't just having the magic, it's knowing what to do with it.' Henrietta's wrinkles were deep with worry. 'Georgie's trained, but only by your mother, and brilliant magician though she is, she was hardly aiming for a rounded education, was she?'

'You think we wouldn't be able to do it?'

'I've heard of Rose Fell,' Henrietta muttered. 'And Mr Fountain, and his daughter. They were strong, strong magicians, Lily. Clever, and *imaginative*. You don't want to meet a creature that Rose Fell dreamed up down some dark prison passageway.'

'Then what do we do?' Lily practically wailed. Archgate had been almost within their grasp, and now it had been snatched away again.

'You need an older magician to teach you.' Henrietta kneaded the quilt with anxious paws. 'But we don't have one, except your father, and we can't get him out of prison without the spells you need to learn first!' She slumped down with her chin on her paws.

A sudden hammering on the door brought her leaping to her feet indignantly, and she barked a warning.

'What is it?' Lily called, stroking Henrietta calm again.

'It's me, Nicholas. Daniel wants you in the audience; he says he needs people to tell him how the act looks from the front.'

Lily sighed. 'All right.'

Daniel was fussing about everything being perfect. The dragon had turned out to have a remarkable sense of pitch, and he kept pointing out exactly which of the musicians were flat. The conductor of the band had already handed in his notice twice. Now the stagehands were taking bets on which of Mary and Nicholas would cry first. By the time Lily and Georgie got to the front of the theatre, both of the new assistants were looking worried.

'It's this cabinet trick,' Mary murmured to Lily, leaning over the front of the stage, while Daniel harangued the scene painters again. 'It does work, but Nicholas and I keep getting mixed up about which of us is supposed to jump out when. And I don't like being shut up in that tiny space with him anyway. I don't trust him not to turn me all green and hairy like that poor rabbit. He might not mean to, but he's nervous, and things go wrong when he's nervous.'

'Is she complaining about me?' Nicholas demanded crossly. 'I bet she is. Girls always blame someone else when they make mistakes.'

'I didn't!' Mary yelped furiously. 'Oh! It was you!' She stamped across the stage, aiming a sharp kick at the Vanishing Cabinet as she went past it. The side of the cabinet promptly fell off, and Mary rushed away from the stage in tears, followed by a gloomy voice from up in the lighting rig.

'All right, William, I know, I owes you a shilling...'

Despite the dramatic end to the rehearsals, the act was still to go ahead. Lily and Georgie had flattered and coaxed Mary into going on, and Daniel had told Nicholas that if he let so much as a speck of real magic pass his lips, he would sell him to a chimney sweep. Then he'd given him sixpence and sent him out to buy sweets, feeling guilty.

'Do you think he'll be all right?' Georgie whispered to Lily in the wings, as they watched Daniel and Nicholas and Mary preparing to go on.

Lily nodded. 'He has to understand how to keep his magic bottled up inside him. With the way things are now, it's the most important thing he has to learn. Even if it feels horrible,' she added sadly. She hated not being able to use her magic whenever she wanted. It felt like pins and needles in her fingers, only ever so much worse.

'What's the matter with his face?' Georgie muttered, a few minutes later, as Nicholas trotted past them to fetch a flaming torch. His cheeks looked swollen, and Lily stifled a laugh.

'Daniel gave him money for sweets, because he'd shouted at him so much. He's got toffee stuffed in both sides, I reckon.'

Even though Nicholas looked like he had severe toothache, the unaccustomed sweetness of the toffee was distracting him from green furry monster-rabbits. He smiled blissfully, and the magic on stage stayed strictly artificial as the act went on.

Mary was even slimmer than Lily, and she looked even more convincingly disappeared inside the Devil's Cabinet. Daniel had added to the Divided Lady trick with a very realistic pair of false feet that Mary had to stick out of the end of the box. It gave the illusion an even more gory feel, and several of the audience stood up and clapped. One lady in a very feathery hat actually fainted.

'It's going so well!' Lily hissed to Nicholas, as he darted into the wings to fetch a silvered hoop for the levitation trick, and he nodded happily.

Georgie watched with professional interest as Mary lay down on the tabletop, her full skirts spilling out over the wooden platform that would lift her high into the air.

'She doesn't look as bewitched as you did,' Lily told her loyally.

Georgie glanced at her gratefully. 'Maybe not. She looks good though; you'd never think it was all a trick, even from the side.'

The levitation was one of the most dramatic parts of the act. Before, Lily had always been part of it, watching Georgie and hoping that she wouldn't slip, or let the board show. She'd been concentrating on her poses, and the delicate hand movements that she usually got wrong. She hadn't watched the audience, or felt them.

Now, standing in the wings, their excitement and delight was reaching out to her in waves. She could feel her magic responding, dancing joyfully inside her. She cast an anxious glance towards Nicholas, but he was focused on the show, and his magic seemed to be under control.

As Mary climbed higher on the lifting apparatus, and Daniel swept the hoop around her to prove that she really was floating – even Lily could hardly see the clever twist he made around the joist that was actually holding her – the audience grew more and more enthralled. Lily turned to stare out into the theatre, smiling at the wide eyes of those in the front few rows. One little girl, dressed in the height of fashion and clearly out past her bedtime for a special treat, was standing up, clapping her plump hands excitedly and then hugging her doll, which was dressed as beautifully as she was.

Lily swallowed suddenly. The little girl was surrounded by a delicate wash of golden light. It ran down the curls of hair, sparkling around her face, and shining in her eyes. Magic.

The girl's mother stared down at her in amazement, and then the child held her hands out in front of her and let go of her fabulous doll. Her mother reached to catch the toy, but dropped her hand back as the doll floated into the air. Just like Mary – except that there was no lifting mechanism concealed behind a curtain. This was an outpouring of perfect, childish power, and no one could deny it.

The golden light around the child and the doll was

already drawing attention. Whispers and gasps ran through the audience, and several people were standing up to see what was happening. People were leaning out of the boxes and pointing.

The little girl's father caught her up swiftly and hurried along the front row of seats, making for the aisle, while she wailed in his arms, demanding her doll back. The mother reached out a tentative hand towards the floating creature, but didn't dare to touch her. She left the pretty toy hanging in the air as she half ran after her husband and daughter. The door at the back of the theatre slammed, and the doll fell to the ground, the golden light seeping away into the faces of the audience.

Daniel drew the act to a close after that, even though it meant leaving out the new Vanishing Cabinet trick. It wasn't the time. As the audience cleared the theatre, Lily could feel the gossip about the strange little incident spreading out across the city as they made for their homes.

The doll still lay forlornly, half under the little girl's seat. No one had wanted to take it, even though it was clearly valuable. Henrietta tugged it out gently by its silken skirt, and Lily crouched down to pick it up. 'It's beautiful. I never had a doll like this. Peter made me a wooden one, once. But this – look at her eyes!'

The doll's eyes rolled open and closed as Lily tipped

her – some clever weighting inside the porcelain head.

'Do you think they'll come back for her?' Lily wondered.

Henrietta snorted. 'Of course they won't! They'll hide that little girl away, and pretend they were never at the theatre. I wouldn't be surprised if that family went travelling on the continent for a while. Magic isn't outlawed in Talis; she'd be safe there.'

'What will happen now?' Georgie whispered above them. She was sitting on the edge of the stage, eyeing the doll anxiously. 'Someone will tell. They're bound to. Or even if they don't report it directly, the gossip will get to the Queen's Men.'

Daniel trudged across the stage, wearily peeling off his false moustache. 'I suppose we shouldn't be surprised. It's been happening in the streets, and the grocer's boy was telling me that someone made a sack of rice explode in the shop the other day. Rice everywhere, and he had to sweep it up. With all the excitement in the audience it was bound to happen sooner or later.' He put an arm around Georgie's shoulders. 'You girls had better get ready to hide.'

FOUR

It was as though the little girl's explosion of magic had opened a door inside the theatre. There was another outbreak the next night, and a coyly worded article in the newspaper followed, giving the name of the theatre and mentioning the Amazing Danieli – Daniel's stage name.

'We're breaking no laws,' Daniel muttered, as he smoothed down the pages with a snap. 'But we've been warned before. This is very dangerous.'

'Surely it must be obvious that this is simply an outpouring of unused magic,' the dragon pointed out. They were all leaning against him, reading the article over Daniel's shoulders. 'What do they expect, after fifty years letting it lie fallow in the ground? Especially here. The land is positively groaning with power.'

Daniel nodded thoughtfully. 'London has always been known as a magical city.'

'Your act speaks to the magic inside others. And it may be worse now that I am here.' The dragon swung his head round to eye Daniel apologetically. 'Dragons are full of magic, and we strengthen others' power.'

Daniel sighed, and nodded. He folded the newspaper carefully and laid it down on the stage. 'Things aren't going to be the same again, are they? Magic is coming back. The Queen's Men think they can root it out, but that's not going to work. The more they stamp it down, the more it will bubble up somewhere else.'

Lily wrapped her arms around Henrietta, feeling her own magic leap inside her with excitement. 'That's what I think too,' she whispered. 'It's going to happen. Maybe not for a little while, but...'

Nicholas hugged Georgie, and then let go very quickly, looking embarrassed. 'Sorry,' he muttered. 'It's just – after all that time at Fell Hall, thinking that magic was dead. It's wonderful...'

'But meanwhile, we're an obvious scapegoat,' Daniel muttered. 'I hate to say this, Lily and Georgie, but you're not safe here. We need to find you somewhere else to hide out. Perhaps the princess as well, although I suppose we can disguise her as any old lady – she sews so well, she'd be convincing as a wardrobe mistress.'

Georgie sighed. That was all she had ever wanted to be, as well.

'But where are they going to go?' the dragon asked, his voice a low, disapproving rumble. 'I do not want them leaving me. They are mine; there's Fell blood in them somewhere. How can I keep them safe, if I'm not with them? There are not many places in this narrow city where I can stay.'

Daniel looked at the girls helplessly. 'I don't know. I've friends that you girls could stay with, but no one has a house large enough for a dragon.' He sighed. 'I'll ask around. All right. Nicholas. You need to come and practise your juggling.' He tucked the paper under his arm, and moved off to the side of the stage, with Nicholas trailing after him, muttering.

'Just a little magic? Couldn't I? Just so the balls would stick to my hands – they're so *slippery*...'

Lily rubbed the dragon's side, trying to seem comforting. His neck was drooping anxiously, and she could feel vibrations of worry coming off his scales. 'It wouldn't be for long, hopefully. Once we've worked out the spells to free Father, we can go wherever we like. We don't have to stay in London. We'll find somewhere with lots of space for dragons.' She glanced at Georgie. 'If we didn't have to worry about Mama, we could even go back to Merrythought. You could fly us there, you'd love it. I'm sure you'd fit; you could sleep in the library, it's enormous.' She looked up at him thoughtfully. 'Our magic was strong enough to wake you... Georgie, don't you think that with his power too we might be able to rescue Father? Even though we don't know all the right magic for the prison guard spells?'

'Talk sense, Lily,' Georgie snapped. 'How are we supposed to stand outside an archway in the middle of London, right outside the palace, with a house-sized dragon, and not have anyone asking us what we're doing? Henrietta's right – for once. It's no good just getting into the prison. We need someone to teach us how to defeat those guards. And there isn't anyone.'

The dragon huffed out a steamy sigh. 'My magic isn't like yours – it isn't spells, it's just a strength. A power. I can't teach you. I could go searching for someone who could...'

'How?' Lily asked.

The dragon's thick scales rippled in a reptilian shrug. 'Fly over the city – I can smell where the magicians are. It shouldn't be too hard to claw one out.'

'You mean, just reach into a house and grab them?' Lily muttered, her eyes widening.

The dragon nodded, and Lily sighed regretfully. 'It would be a bit obvious. And I suppose that anyone we did that to might not want to teach us anything afterwards.'

The dragon shrugged again. 'I could command them to,' he suggested.

'Not a strong magician, like we need,' Georgie broke in. 'Someone like your old Fell masters. Could you?'

The dragon shook the spiny ruffs around his head irritably. 'Perhaps not,' he admitted eventually.

'Maybe you could search us out a magician, and then we'd know the house, and we could simply go and ask?' Georgie wondered. 'We'd have to have some sort of excuse. They'd be hiding their magic; it would be dangerous.'

Henrietta sniffed. 'Everything about this is dangerous. *She* is dangerous.' She pressed her cold, damp nose against Georgie's stockinged leg, which she knew quite well Georgie hated.

'Tonight then, after the performance.' The dragon stretched out his wings in pleasure. 'Will you fly with me, dear ones?'

'Lily!'

Lily glanced round, expecting that Sam wanted her to help with something. Nicholas had forgotten one of the props, perhaps, or someone had lost a vital part of their costume. Now that she wasn't going on stage, everyone was borrowing her to run errands. She'd been dragging Peter around with her too, showing him where everything was and making the rest of the theatre folk see that he was still useful, even if he couldn't speak. She'd explained lip-reading too, over and over, and it seemed to be starting to work. Peter was curled up in a corner of the wings now, deftly unpicking a tangle of ropes that someone had given him.

At least, he had been. Now he'd cast the ropes down and was standing, fists clenched, staring out of the wings to the passage beyond.

Lily turned round slowly to follow his gaze.

'Lily, you have to hurry,' Sam muttered. 'No, it's too late. Where's your sister?'

'What is it?' Lily started towards him, but he waved her back.

'No!'

Henrietta darted quickly out into the passageway. 'I'll fetch her. The princess too.'

'Why?' Lily would have stamped her foot, if the act hadn't been going on a few feet away. 'What's happening?'

'Queen's Men...' Sam was turning anxiously this way and that, as though he was sniffing them out. 'Here, you.' He beckoned to Peter. 'Out to the yard, you getting me? Out and check if they've surrounded us.'

Peter nodded grimly, and slid into the passageway.

'You could slip out into the audience, but you'd have to get down the steps from the stage – you'd be spotted.'

Peter hurried back into the wings, grimacing and holding up his notebook. *All gates manned. Coming!*

Georgie tumbled after him, leading Princess Jane, who suddenly looked to Lily unmistakeably a princess, as though the Queen's Men couldn't possibly mistake her for anything else.

She'd been panicking until then, unsure what to do, how to escape, her feet leaden and slow. But she would not let them take the old lady back and seal her up for who-knew-how-many-more years.

'We can't get out!' Georgie hissed. 'They're searching all the rooms, everywhere, there's hundreds of them!'

On stage, Daniel, Nicholas and Mary were reaching the finale of the act – the Vanishing Cabinet. The dragon was coiled decoratively across the back of the stage, looking as much like fabric stretched over wire as he possibly could. But he was staring directly at Lily, and she could see his barbed tail pointing towards the audience. The Queen's Men were there too. The huge dark eyes were questioning, and she gazed back into them, trying to hear him. At Fell Hall, he had been able to speak directly into her mind, but he had lived there for hundreds of years – the very air had been his to bend and shape.

Now, at last, she heard him faintly.

Fly with you? Break out of the front wall? Could be done...

Lily shook her head firmly. However strong he was, she didn't think it would work, not here.

Besides, she had another plan.

On stage, Daniel was starting to work his way gradually towards the wings. He could see the dark-uniformed men moving around the sides of the auditorium, and he knew what they were. He was trying to get back to Lily and Georgie, to find some way to help without the Queen's Men realising what he was doing.

'Bring the cabinet over here!' she hissed to him, as he continued his magician's patter, strolling in wide circles around the stage, making strange magical gestures with his arms, and on every turn, coming closer to her.

He blinked as he heard her, and then raised his eyebrows slightly.

'Please!' she whispered. 'I've got a plan.'

'Have you?' Georgie muttered anxiously. 'What are we going to do?'

'It's a Vanishing Cabinet,' Lily whispered back. 'We're going to vanish in it.'

Georgie stared at her as though she thought Lily had lost her wits. 'It's a fake! It doesn't vanish people, Lily, it's a trick, you know that!'

'This time it will,' Lily told her stubbornly.

On stage, Daniel was directing Nicholas and Mary to move the Vanishing Cabinet around so that all the audience could see that it had no secret back door. 'My rivals have been heard to say the Cabinet is placed exactly over a hole in the floor of the stage,' he told the audience, striding up and down in front of the wooden box as Mary and Nicholas pushed it almost into the wings. 'Or that we have a secret passage out of the back of the theatre! Nonsense, of course. This is a true Vanishing Cabinet – built of wood from a rare Arabian tree, now almost completely extinct.'

He was making it all up off the top of his head, Lily could tell, busking to buy them some time. She pulled Georgie and the princess into the Cabinet after her, and nodded to Mary and Nicholas that it was safe to pull it out to the front of the stage again.

The Cabinet smelled of wood shavings and the sickly whiff of varnish. As Mary carefully shut the door, Daniel's voice was muffled. Lily could only half hear as he explained to the audience that his young assistants were going to disappear.

'Lily, in less than a minute he's going to open the door for Mary and Nicholas to get in, and everyone will see us!' Henrietta growled. 'We won't all fit into the secret compartment, it's too tight. I hope you have a plan.'

'We're going to vanish. The dragon will help us. He will. He'll have to.' Lily closed her eyes.'

'Er, where are we going to vanish to?' Georgie asked.

Lily opened her eyes again, and swallowed. But it didn't help the strange blockage in her throat. 'I don't know!' Her voice wavered, and all of a sudden her plan seemed stupid and dangerous. 'We have to go now, and I don't know where we're going!'

'I know somewhere.' Princess Jane took Lily's hand in hers. Lily could feel her fine old bones as brittle as sticks inside the papery skin, but her grip was determined and reassuring. 'How do we get there?'

Lily gulped. 'Just think of it. Think of it hard. Georgie, hold hands. It's all right, I won't use your magic; I know we can't risk it.' Hurriedly, she scooped Henrietta up, and tucked the little dog into the crook of one arm.

She could feel Georgie's magic seething excitedly deep inside her, her sister's own power mixed with the strange, dark spells their mother had implanted in her. The spells felt even stronger than they had before. She darted away from them, searching instead for the dragon's magic, hoping that he would lend it to her again. It came to her in a sudden surge, lifting her own magic with it, so that it felt as though she were flying with him again.

Clinging to Princess Jane's frail fingers, Lily borrowed the sense of safety from the old lady's thoughts. There was a memory of warmth, and sunlight, and buttered scones, and Lily let out a sad sort of laugh. The only place she felt safe was here, at the theatre, and even that refuge had been stolen away from them now.

From somewhere far away, she felt Nicholas's anxious fingers on the handle of the Cabinet, as he wondered if it was safe to open it. With a fraction of the magic that was spinning through her, Lily loosed the catch so that the door swung open with an eerie creak, revealing only an empty space.

'Where are we?' Georgie whispered, a few moments later.

'I don't know. I went to the place Miss Jane said. I think we're here. I'm almost sure we are.' Lily shivered. The princess had filled her mind with sunlit memories, but this was a dark September evening, and there was a chill wind seeping through the little building they were sitting in.

'We are here…' Princess Jane's voice was shaking, and Lily pressed close against her, wrapping her arms around the old lady. Henrietta clambered into her lap and curled up protectively.

'I can smell flowers,' Georgie said doubtfully.

'Roses,' the princess agreed. 'There was a climbing

rose over the roof. It can't be the same one, all this time later. A cutting, perhaps.'

There was a faint sound of water splashing and falling, and a pigeon was murmuring contentedly somewhere overhead. Lily blinked, her vision adjusting in the evening light. They were sitting in some small space, and a much, much larger building was looming up in front of them.

'Is that the palace?' she asked in a very small voice.

She felt Princess Jane nod, as though she didn't trust her voice.

'It's so long since I've been here,' the old lady whispered at last. 'It's a summerhouse, in the gardens. I used to sit here to sew. Hardly anyone ever came here, Lily, I promise you. We won't be found.'

'Are you sure?' Georgie murmured, peering out anxiously into the darkness. 'Your mother must be over there somewhere – she hates us!'

'Perhaps it was a stupid place to bring you,' the princess said apologetically. 'It was my place, you see; I always felt safe here. When you asked for somewhere safe, Lily, I could feel this spot, deep inside me.'

'Then it's probably the right place,' Henrietta muttered, leaping down from her lap and nosing her way to the open double doors. 'Instinct is very important, and all too often you humans don't listen to it.' She sniffed cautiously, and then looked back up at them all, her round, dark eyes glinting in the moonlight. 'But I have to tell you, someone's coming.'

'Who?' Georgie demanded anxiously.

Henrietta scraped her claws on the boarded floor irritably. 'I'm a dog, Georgiana, not a mind-reader. I don't know! One person. With several others following at a distance. A woman, oldish. Wearing a very strong scent of gardenias – ugh, she must have poured it on with a ladle!'

Princess Jane chuckled. 'Sophia always wore too much of it; Charlotte and I would tease her.'

'Your sister? The queen?' Lily squeaked, and Henrietta hissed at her warningly.

'Sssshhhh! She's close!' The pug cocked her head to one side. 'But I don't expect she heard you. I think she's crying.'

Lily and Georgie could hear her now too, light footsteps pacing up and down the gravelled path, pattering and scrunching. And a voice whispering sadly, interspersed with little sobbing catches of breath.

'What's she crying for?' Lily muttered. 'She's a *queen*, how can she be so unhappy?'

Georgie shook her head. 'Don't you remember when we saw her in that parade? How worried she looked?'

'I suppose,' Lily whispered back. Since then she'd

been stolen away by the queen's own force of guards, and she wasn't feeling as sympathetic as she had been before.

'Poor Sophia…' Princess Jane stood up, and Lily caught at her skirt anxiously.

'Don't! You can't!'

'But she's crying…' The princess tried to pull away, but froze as another set of footsteps trod sharply into the garden.

'Sophia!' The voice was older, cracked-sounding, and Jane stepped back into the shadows, pressing herself against the back wall of the little summerhouse.

'My mother…' she whispered, the words hardly more than a breath, and the four of them huddled onto the bench seat, clinging silently to each other in the darkness.

FIVE

ventually, Queen Adelaide led her daughter and their bodyguards out of the garden, leaving the girls and the princess clinging together inside the summerhouse.

'Did you hear?' Lily whispered. 'She thinks her mother is being too strict.'

'I knew Sophia wasn't behind the way the Queen's Men are behaving now,' Princess Jane murmured. 'She couldn't have changed so much, even after all these years.'

'But your mother is in charge now, isn't she?' Henrietta pointed out. 'She's the Queen Regent. It makes no difference what Queen Sophia thinks.'

'Is it for ever? Can't they change it back?' Lily asked, frowning.

Henrietta grunted. 'Not to be unfeeling –' here she nudged Princess Jane with a wet nose – 'but the old queen won't last that much longer, will she? She must be in her eighties.'

Princess Jane sighed. 'She looked awfully healthy to me. I can be just as unfeeling as you, Henrietta dear. I have very little affection for my mother, after forty years shut away on her orders.'

'Who is your sister's heir?' Georgie asked suddenly.

'Our next sister, Lucasta, and our little sister, Charlotte, both had to give up their claim to the throne when they married foreign royalty,' the princess explained.

'But that only leaves you!' Lily gasped.

'Well, except that I'm dead,' the princess sighed. 'Officially. I expect the heir is some distant cousin now.'

'You'd be a much better queen,' Lily muttered. 'And I don't care if that *is* treachery, and sedition, and all those things. Once we've got Father back and mended Georgie, I think we should fight for you to be restored to the throne.'

The princess smiled at her. 'I think you can probably be beheaded for saying things like that. But I have had an idea, about freeing your father.'

'Really?' Lily sat up eagerly. 'I was planning that we could sneak back to the theatre and get the dragon, then he could still try and sniff us out a magician to help, like he suggested. But I'm still not sure any magician is actually going to want to help us; it's too dangerous.'

'I think I know one who will. But you'll have to go and find her.'

'Who?' Lily breathed, and Georgie caught the princess's hand excitedly.

'The girl I told you about while we were still at Fell Hall. Rose, the apprentice magician who was my bodyguard. She was an orphan, a foundling. But then she found her mother in the end, and discovered that in fact she was a Fell, a child with a great magical heritage. She was one of the greatest magicians in London – she was truly famous. She and her master, Aloysius Fountain, helped to design the Archgate spells. So why not ask her to help you defeat them?'

'Do you think she would?' Lily and Georgie spoke at once.

'And more importantly, where is she?' Henrietta demanded.

'She went to America, after the Decree,' Princess Jane said sadly. 'She fought against it for a long time – Mr Fountain did as well. He was Chief Counsellor to the Treasury, an important government post, before the queen had him dismissed. He was an alchemist, you see; he could make gold. But no one listened to them, or to me. Everyone was whipped up into such a fury. All magicians were traitors, all magic was suspect. And so they left.' Tears were running down the princess's face as she remembered her friends. 'She went to live in New York. She wrote to me – told me how lovely it was. They were destitute, as my dear sister had seized the property of any magicians who fled the country, but Rose's magic was much admired over there. She built up a business with Mr Fountain, prospecting for gold. Telling people where to dig their mines. And then she got married.' Here the princess sniffed delicately, as though she didn't quite approve. 'Rather beneath her, I always thought, to marry a servant boy, but she was very happy.'

'So we'd have to travel to America?' Georgie asked doubtfully.

Lily nodded, staring out into the darkness. 'How would we get there? Oh! Colette's going to America! To New York, don't you remember? She told us, the very first night we came back to the theatre. She's going to sing on board a steam ship, a great ocean liner.'

'And do you know how much a passage on one of those ships costs?' Georgie snapped. 'Maria told me. Pounds! Colette couldn't afford it, that's why she's working her passage! We haven't got the money, Lily, and even if we could borrow it from Daniel, you need papers to travel on a ship like that. We're fugitives, remember?'

Lily scowled. 'We could find some way. Couldn't we buy fake papers? And we could disguise ourselves, like we did when we first arrived in London. Don't you want to get these spells lifted?'

'Of course I do,' Georgie muttered. 'But we don't even know if she's still there. She might be anywhere by now – it was forty years ago.'

'Even if this Rose has gone, America would still be a good place to find a magician to help you,' Henrietta pointed out. 'Magic is perfectly acceptable over there, and a great many of the magicians who went into exile fled to New York, or so Daniel told me. You're sure to find someone who knows your family, someone who'd want to help rescue your father.' She rubbed her velvety muzzle on Lily's hand. 'And even if you don't, you're safer there than here.'

'I am,' Lily murmured. 'What would happen to Georgie?'

'The further away she is from your mother the better. Your mother can't call on the spells inside Georgie if she's on the other side of the Atlantic, can she?'

'I suppose not,' Lily said thoughtfully. 'What do you think?' She found Georgie's chilly hand and squeezed it.

'I still think we'll be lucky to find her. But I'll try

anything, if we only we can work out some way to get there.' Georgie sighed. 'I could feel the spells inside me, when the queen came close. They knew her. They know what they're for.'

Lily swallowed. They hadn't told Princess Jane what the spells inside Georgie were meant to do, just that they were trying to control her, and hurt her, and that they had to get rid of them.

But the princess put her hands around theirs. 'It's a plot, isn't it? Your mama is a renegade magician – what else would she be fighting for? Georgie is a weapon.' She laughed. 'My poor dear mother. So convinced that every magician is up to no good. If they weren't before, they certainly are now, after all her harsh treatment.'

'You don't hate me?' Georgie whispered.

'No. But I think it's your duty to do anything you can to free yourself of these spells. You *must* go and search out Rose.'

'Can we really go back the same way?' Georgie whispered.

'I hope so.' Lily looked anxiously out into the dark gardens. It felt very late, so late that she was sure she could see the sky lightening over behind the trees. She had a feeling that the palace gardeners would be at work early, and they couldn't risk being discovered.

'What if they left guards at the theatre?' Georgie insisted anxiously.

'What if we all get lost halfway there and end up on the moon?' Henrietta snarled. 'Stop what-iffing! We don't know! Do you want to stay here? Then we'll be caught by the Queen's Men for certain, won't we?'

'I was only trying—' Georgie began furiously.

'Be quiet!'

Georgie and Henrietta fell silent at once, the pug's jaws closing with a definite snap, and Lily stared at the princess admiringly. Was it a special sort of magic, to be able to command people like that? Or was it just something that princesses learned?

'Lily. Take us back, please.' The princess stood up, and took both girls' hands. 'We are all tired and frightened. But that is no excuse for quarrelling.'

Henrietta scrabbled at Lily's leg to be picked up, and nestled quietly into her shoulder. 'I didn't want to ask in front of your sister, but have you enough magic to take us back, without the dragon to help?' she whispered.

'I hope so,' Lily muttered back. 'We'll see, won't we?' She squared her shoulders, trying to summon up all the strength she could. They hadn't really slept, just dozed a little, resting uncomfortably on the wooden benches. They could probably have gone back to the theatre earlier, but they hadn't known how long the Queen's

Men might stay at the theatre searching for them. All the excitement of their escape had drained away now, and Lily felt limp and tired. For once, her magic wasn't bubbling eagerly just under her skin, desperate to be called. She had to search for it, and it felt as tired as she was.

Perhaps they should just stay a little longer? She could sleep, perhaps, and draw back some strength. But then Henrietta tensed against her arm. 'I can hear someone coming. They're whistling!' she muttered. 'We need to go now, Lily.'

Lily dragged the magic up out of her bones and moaned wearily, trying to concentrate on the theatre. Her thoughts seemed to be spiralling round and round inside her head, and she slumped forward.

Princess Jane gripped her hand more tightly, and Georgie flung her arm around Lily's waist. 'It's all right,' she gasped. 'You should have said you were too worn out, idiot. Oh, Lily, I can't help, or we'll end up with another wolf, or something else awful!'

'Think of the theatre,' Henrietta yapped.

Lily was trying, hauling up memories of their act, and the excitement of the performance; how clever Henrietta was with her tricks; Georgie pretending to be entranced – except that one time when she really had been unconscious... No. Lily shuddered and pushed that thought away quickly. Daniel, then, who had rescued them off the street and let them stay, who was running the whole theatre when he wasn't that much older than Georgie, who loved magic so much that he was risking everything by hiding a dragon in plain sight across the back of his stage. The cleverness of the illusions, the new Vanishing Cabinet… She was so tired…

'It's working!' Georgie squeaked.

Lily's eyes jerked open for a second, and she saw the darkness of the summerhouse turn misty and grey around them as they went somewhere else. But she really had no idea where. It felt like that delicious moment just as she fell asleep, where everything faded away. Except that the aching sense that something wasn't right stayed with her.

'Lily!'

A sharp pain jerked her awake again, gasping, and Lily shook her head, unsure what had happened. They weren't in the palace gardens any longer – the faint chirping of waking birds had been replaced by a deep, soft silence, and it was utterly dark. Her ear throbbed, and she could feel a trickle of wetness running down her neck.

'I'm sorry, I'm sorry,' Henrietta wailed. 'But I couldn't think of any other way.'

'You bit her!' Georgie sounded horrified.

'I had to. Lily, wake up, where are we?'

Lily laughed wearily. 'We're vanished. We're nowhere. Where does the audience think Nicholas and Mary go to, when they disappear out of that cabinet?'

'No one knows...' Georgie said faintly. 'Just – somewhere.'

'Well, we're somewhere, then.'

'The air smells bad, here.' Henrietta wriggled uncomfortably. 'There isn't enough of it. Lily, unless you want me to bite you again, and harder, take us back to the theatre. Now.'

'Stupid, reckless children!' someone shouted suddenly, and there was a sharp flash of light before they landed in a tangled knot in the middle of the stage.

The dragon was standing over them, his sides heaving and his scales glowing with a burning silvery light. Each scale seemed to sparkle at the edges, like the facets of a precious stone, and his eyes were fiery.

'What were you doing?' he snarled, clawing them upright none too gently. 'I nearly lost you – a few steps further and I would never have been able to haul you back.'

'We were lost,' Lily muttered, pressing her hand to her bleeding ear. 'I'm sorry, I was so tired I couldn't find the magic to bring us back here, and I was trying so hard to remember where we were going. All I could think of was the act, and the vanishing cabinet, and somehow I vanished us.'

'Travelling by magic is one of the most advanced enchantments,' the dragon hissed, coiling himself around and around them so that his scales flashed blurrily in the backs of Lily's eyes. He darted his head towards the girls, sniffing at them anxiously. 'You must never try it without being certain where you're going, and even more importantly, *when*. You could have ended up somewhere before time, and then where would you be?'

Lily giggled out of pure tiredness, and he snapped his massive teeth at her and then shuddered, all down his great length, and slumped to the stage so heavily that the boards shook and a curtain of dust shimmered down from the high ceiling. 'You laugh, but only because you do not understand,' he growled, his head turned away.

Lily sank down next to him, resting her head on one of his forelegs. 'I know I don't. I wasn't really laughing. I'm just so tired I couldn't help it. And I didn't want to travel by magic – we had to escape and we couldn't do anything else!'

'I could have flown you out of here and taken you somewhere safe,' the dragon muttered stubbornly, glancing back over his shoulder. 'You shouldn't have gone.'

'Only if you'd broken down the walls of the theatre!'

Georgie pointed out. 'And then loads of people would have seen you. Daniel would have had half a theatre left, and the Queen's Men breathing down his neck, wanting to know why he was harbouring criminals. They'd probably have arrested *everyone*!'

The dragon snorted irritably, but was clearly unable to think of an answer. 'You need someone to teach you,' he hissed at last, turning back to face them and letting trails of smoke snake out over the stage. 'I don't know enough about humans and magic – and everything has changed since I last knew an apprentice. We must find you someone. You aren't safe, wandering around untaught. Particularly being as strong as you are.'

Lily nodded. 'We know. We're going to. Princess, *Miss* Jane, I mean, thinks we should go to America, and find a magician she knows.'

The dragon's eyes hooded thoughtfully. 'America? That new-found land?' Then he sighed. 'I suppose it isn't, any longer. Someone you trust?' he demanded sharply, turning to the princess, who had seated herself wearily on a small gilt chair that the acrobats used for balancing.

She smiled at him. 'Indeed. And you will too. A Fell. Rose Fell.'

He brightened at once, even his scales shimmering more strongly. 'Ah, well! In that case… But I do not think I can fly that far…' he muttered, staring down at his lethal claws, as he couldn't meet their eyes. 'Not yet. I am not up to my old strength, still. Halfway, perhaps.'

Lily shook her head. 'I hadn't even thought of asking you to fly us. We're going to try and get aboard a ship, though we aren't sure how.' She yawned. 'We'll talk to Colette, later on…'

The dragon nodded his great head, and then stretched out his neck and twitched a folded drape out from behind the curtains, flicking it out so that it crumpled and nested between his forelegs. 'You can sleep there. I want to know where you are. Especially if you're about to travel to the other side of the world without me.'

'Will it really work?' Lily asked doubtfully, staring down at the trunk. The space looked tight, tighter even than the illusion cabinets.

Sam shrugged. 'Can't see why not. Why would they be suspicious?'

'I suppose.' Lily frowned, wriggling her shoulders, and turned to Colette. 'Will you unpack them quickly? Please?'

Henrietta sniffed. 'She'll have to be careful, Lily. It would be suspicious if she went to unpack right away.' She jumped up, resting her front paws on the edge of the open trunk and sniffing at the false bottom and the hiding place underneath. 'She'll want to take me for a walk up and down the deck first, I should think. That's what someone who didn't have two stowaways in their luggage would do.'

Lily scowled. 'I think it would be better if you hid away with me. You're too recognisable.'

Henrietta shook her head briskly. 'No one's ever seen me with Colette. And I don't do well in confined spaces. Not after however many years it was being a painting. I come over all peculiar inside, and you certainly wouldn't want to be shut up with me.'

Georgie groaned in disgust, and then gave Lily a last hug. 'Make sure you've labelled them properly, won't you?' she begged Colette. 'Cabin baggage. I really don't want to end up in the hold.' She stepped quickly into the trunk and lay down, fussily arranging her skirts so that they wouldn't crease.

'I've drilled holes in this, Miss Georgie,' Sam assured her, as he slid the board over her, and Lily shivered. The thought of being shut away in the dark was even worse after their strange adventure three days ago. What if when she couldn't see, she found she couldn't feel either, and she was back in that dark emptiness between the worlds?

'Lily. Daniel's already gone to call a hansom cab. And

Colette needs to be able to put her costumes in on top of you. It has to be now.' Sam wrapped his arms around her, smelling comfortably of pipe tobacco and gravy, and she kissed his whiskery cheek.

'I know.' She lay down, screwing her eyes closed so as not to see him shutting her in, and took an experimental breath. The air was hot, and a little dusty, but it was there. She didn't need to scream.

'Lifting you now,' Sam muttered. 'Don't you talk. We'll be taking you out to the carriage, you can't let the driver suspect anything.'

Lily nodded, and then realised that no one could see her.

'It's like the theatre, only ten times more so,' Georgie muttered. 'And it isn't painted on a canvas flat, it's real.'

Lily nodded. The ship was so large that Colette had told them they needn't remain hidden in her room, as they'd expected they might have to. There were a great many other children, and provided they didn't make themselves too obvious, she was sure that no one would suspect the girls weren't meant to be on board. Luckily, she had been given a first-class cabin, so as to be closer to the room where she was to perform, and so there was room enough for Lily and Georgie to sleep on the little sofa and the padded seat below the porthole. Colette was very good at sneaking food into her bag for them from meals – she said that Daniel had taught her sleight of hand.

The *Marianna* was one of the newest ocean liners, fitted out to be more of a floating hotel than a ship. It was due to take only six days to steam to New York, and the passengers – or at least the first class-ones – were spending those days in petted luxury. The ship's crew seemed to spend most of their time answering silly questions from passengers and very little time actually sailing the ship, as far as Lily could see. Henrietta wasn't the only animal on board, either. The promenade deck was full of fussy little lapdogs, and one elderly first-class passenger had brought her parrot, which had already escaped twice, and they'd only been sailing for a day and a half.

One of the ship's stewards had already been forced to explain to Mrs Archibald that the parrot must stay in her cabin this evening, which she was very indignant about. But other passengers had objected to his trying to join in with last night's musical soiree – he seemed to be convinced that he was a tenor, and he let out ear-splitting squawks to join in with all the high notes. Mrs Archibald was now sitting in one of the armchairs at the front of the gilded music room, glowering and making life difficult for the waiters by insisting on particular sorts of tea leaves that they didn't have.

Lily and Georgie were lurking in the least popular chairs at the side of the music room, trying to look as though they were meant to be there. If anyone asked, they were planning to say that Colette had asked them to look after Henrietta, who was enjoying shipboard life far too much to stay in the cabin. Lily was slightly worried that all the attention and compliments she was receiving were going to go to her head, and she would forget herself and ask the next admiring lady to scratch her behind the other ear, please.

'Is that a real tree?' Georgie asked, staring at an enormous palm apparently growing from the floor, and Henrietta helpfully trotted over to sniff at it. 'Yes,' she whispered, putting her front paws up on Lily's lap. 'There's a pot set into the carpet.' She whisked down again and began to thread her way around the assembled passengers, begging prettily and accepting lump sugar and bonbons.

'It's like that Arabian Nights backdrop they had at the theatre for the Eastern jugglers. I wonder if Queen Sophia's palace is like this inside,' Lily muttered, starting to clap as Colette emerged to sing.

Luckily, Colette was very popular with the passengers – she had mixed enough bits of opera into her usual act to make everyone feel cultured and highbrow, and the purser had asked her to add an afternoon concert as well as the evenings she had been booked for.

'Which is all very well,' she told Georgie anxiously as they crept back into her cabin after her concert. Luckily they could use Henrietta to stand guard at the end of the passageway, so no one saw them going into someone else's cabin. 'But with you two in my trunks, I haven't brought as many costumes as I should have done. I'll need to adapt some of my dresses; I can't wear the same one twice.'

'We'll help,' Lily told her, feeling guilty, especially as she really meant that Georgie would – Lily would be worse than useless.

'Did you see that old lady in the front row of chairs?' Henrietta asked. 'The cross one?'

'What, the parrot lady?' Colette smiled. 'Of course. I could borrow some costumes from her, perhaps. That purplish hair has to be a wig.'

Henrietta sniffed thoughtfully. 'I thought so too. Well. Not a wig. But certainly not real.'

Lily stared at her. 'What are you talking about?'

Henrietta leaped up onto the armchair, and arranged herself in her best china dog pose, the way she always did when she had something important to say. 'She isn't right. I couldn't get quite close enough, but there's something odd about her.'

Georgie shook her head irritably. 'Well, of course there is, she's travelling across the Atlantic with that dreadful parrot.'

'I'm not that convinced about the parrot either,' Henrietta said, glancing at Lily with her head on one side. 'It didn't smell right – it doesn't smell at all, in fact, which is unnatural. Most parrots stink. And when those two stewards were chasing it down A deck this morning, it didn't shed any feathers.'

Lily swallowed. 'Is she under a glamour? Like Aunt Clara?'

Henrietta scratched one ear delicately with a hind paw. 'Ah!' She gave the ear a luxurious little shake. 'Mmmm. Possibly.'

Colette was frowning. 'A glamour? That's like a disguise, isn't it? So the parrot is actually what – a pigeon?' She was smiling, as though she thought this was all rather funny, but Lily had a horrible feeling it wasn't.

'It doesn't smell of pigeon either.' Henrietta blinked at Lily solemnly, her round eyes owl-like. 'Seems to me more like some sort of construct. It may well have been a parrot *once*. Or possibly a pigeon. A dead one.'

'So it's something like Marten then.' Lily didn't really want to say it. If she said it, it might be true. She shivered. Her mother had created her own strange, dark servant, back at Merrythought. A tangle of spells and borrowed flesh, that she had sent chasing after Lily and Georgie when they escaped the island. 'That sort of spell-construct is very difficult, you told us. And terribly rare. You have to have a talent for it; most people never could make anything like that.'

'Most people would never want to,' Henrietta snapped. 'But yes.'

'What are you two trying to say?' Georgie stood up, her face whitish in the fierce electric glare of the cabin lights.

Lily sighed, and went over to her sister, wrapping her arms around her. Georgie was shaking. 'We're saying that Mrs Archibald definitely isn't who she says she is. She's almost certainly got a glamour on, and she has a pet parrot that's actually some sort of spell-flesh. And the only person we know who can do that is our mother.'

Georgie sagged in her arms. 'She's following us!' she whispered.

Henrietta shook her head. 'No. She hasn't shown any interest in you two, or Colette. And she didn't even seem to notice me!' Henrietta sounded rather indignant about this. 'Marten saw me in London, even if your mother never did, and I am quite recognisable. No. This is just luck – good or bad, I'm not sure which.'

Georgie lifted her head from Lily's shoulder and gaped at the dog. 'How could it be good luck? She's hunting us!'

Henrietta sniffed. 'You, actually. And I think she may have given up on you for the moment. She must have some other plan. Perhaps this plot to assassinate the

Queen has co-conspirators in New York? Or maybe she just wants to live somewhere that she doesn't have to hide her magic. Perhaps she's given up on the plot.'

Lily shook her head. 'I don't believe that at all.'

Henrietta nodded. 'No, maybe not. But it is good luck that we've spotted her then. We want to know where she is and what she's doing, don't we?'

'We have to stay out of her way,' Lily murmured anxiously. 'You especially, Georgie.' She pushed her sister down on the little sofa and sat next to her, eyeing her sternly. 'If you get too close to her, she'll be able to sense those spells. And they might sense her too.'

'I don't understand why she has to go to the bother of disguising herself,' Colette said, frowning, as she began to remove her make-up at the ornate dressing table. 'Ugh, this lighting makes me look haggard. I much prefer gas lamps. If she's such a powerful magician, can't she just fly herself to New York, or something like that? She must have had to fake papers too, to get on the ship.'

Lily exchanged a glance with Georgie, remembering their own attempt at travelling by magic. 'It's exhausting, trying to do something like that. And the same with her glamour. Mama could probably convince everyone on the ship that she was an alligator if she wanted to, but it would take a lot more magic than just being a grumpy old lady. People expect old ladies like Mrs Archibald on ships, I think. And the parrot distracts people, if her glamour slips at all. Anyway, the fake papers might not have been too difficult. Mama wrote letters to other magicians in hiding all the time, didn't she, Georgie? They were all plotting together, Penelope and Cora Dysart told us that. If she's joined up with the other old magical families like the Dysarts, she could probably have a whole ship to herself if she wanted. Jonathan Dysart is one of the queen's favourites, isn't he?'

Colette nodded. 'I've heard of him. But he's not a magician, Lily. He's always talking about how magic is a corrupting influence on society. He was in the paper, saying it ought to be stamped out once and for all.'

Lily snorted. 'He is. He's just brilliant at hiding it. And his daughters are a pair of sweet-faced little beasts. They were the ones who had us sent to Fell Hall.' She shivered. 'If Mama has talked to them, she'll know that Aunt Clara was hiding us at her house.'

There was silence in the velvety room for a moment.

'What do you think she would do?' Georgie whispered. 'It isn't that I really liked Aunt Clara, but I don't want her to be...well, to have bits of her made into another parrot, maybe. And I *do* like Louis.'

Louis was the girls' cousin, a sulky, standoffish boy. They had all thoroughly disliked each other to start with, but eventually Louis had realised that his mother was hiding her own magic, and that he might have inherited it from her. He'd helped Henrietta to escape from Aunt Clara's house so she could chase after the girls on their way to Fell Hall.

'Perhaps we could write to him,' Georgie suggested rather helplessly. 'Send him a warning.'

'It's a bit late for that,' Lily said sadly. 'Maybe Mr Dysart didn't tell Mama about us – I'm not even sure he really knew who we were. It was Cora and Penelope who got us taken away; he just had to go along with it.'

'You had better keep to the cabin for the rest of the journey,' Colette said worriedly. 'I can watch out for Mrs Archibald. Perhaps I can find out where she's going to stay in New York, or if she's travelling on somewhere else.'

Lily frowned. It seemed cowardly just to hide away in the cabin, but if it really was only chance that they had ended up on the same ship as Mama, it would be stupid to risk her catching Georgie again. 'You'd better be careful,' she told Colette seriously. 'She might look like a dotty old lady right now, but she's as mad as a box of frogs. She doesn't care if anyone gets hurt, as long as she gets what she wants. She filled Georgie up with the worst kind of magic, remember, starting when she was tiny. And we're pretty sure she killed both our sisters,' Lily added with a gulp. 'She'll do anything, she really will.'

'I wonder if I could sneak into her room,' Henrietta said thoughtfully.

Georgie and Lily both turned to stare at her. 'Are you mad?'

'Short of Colette wandering up to her after a concert and just happening to ask why she's going to New York and who she's meeting, how else are we going to find out?' Henrietta gave an irritable little growl.

'If Marten saw you, then Mama knows about you,' Lily told her stubbornly. 'She might not have noticed a black pug on the ship, but if she sees you hanging around her room, she's going to remember!'

Henrietta slumped down on the chair, her nose on her paws. 'I suppose,' she muttered. She breathed loud, whistly dog-sighs for a while and then sat up again, her eyes sparkling. 'You could glamour me, Lily! I could be a wolfhound! I've always wondered what it would be like to be tall.'

'Wolfhounds aren't exactly made for sneaking about,' Georgie said, rather unkindly. 'You'd be even more obvious than usual.'

'But it's a good idea...' Lily stood up, pacing thoughtfully round the cabin. 'Except *I'll* do it. I'll glamour myself to look like the maid that cleans Mama's room.'

'I thought we were keeping to the cabin and keeping out of her way!' Georgie wailed.

'You need to. But I've not got spells in me that she'll recognise, have I? She hardly ever saw me at Merrythought, and I'll be glamoured anyway. We might be able to find out what she's doing, Georgie. We need to know.'

'We need not to be dead, or worse!' Georgie said. Her voice softened. 'Lily, maybe we shouldn't even try to find her. Maybe we should just run away, go off and make our fortunes in America like this Rose did. It's a big place. Couldn't we just stay out of Mama's way?'

Lily wrapped an arm round her. 'I'd like that too. But I don't think Mama's come here because she's given up, Georgie. It's part of the plot. I bet Henrietta's right – she's come to find more magicians to join in. I know we think Mama's mad, but our family's famous, the name means a lot to people like us. And I think Mama could be very persuasive. We can't let her drag anyone else into the plot. Besides, we promised Miss Jane.'

'But I promised her that I'd look after you, too,' Georgie sighed. 'And now you're about to walk into Mama's rooms and start spying. I wish we'd never got into all of this.'

'We didn't have a choice. We were born into it, weren't we? I promise, once we've taken the spells out of you, you can be as boring as you like. You can work at the theatre and you never even need to look at another spell.' Lily shook her head at the thought of it. She'd never thought they would end up travelling to America, but now she was secretly looking forward to it. She would be able to do any magic she liked, without hiding it away! She could feel the magic dancing in her blood just with the thought. 'But we have to do this first, before you can settle down.' She looked anxiously at Georgie. Her sister's white-blonde hair was trailing across her face, and she couldn't see her eyes. But she suspected Georgie was crying.

'I know all that really,' Georgie whispered at last. 'It doesn't make it any easier.' She shook her hair back, and tried to look determined. 'So how are we going to do it?'

'Well, at least on a ship there are times for things. We know when she goes to dinner.'

'The parrot doesn't,' Georgie reminded her. 'Not after the incident with the green beans. But she always takes a walk on the promenade deck in the mornings. And the parrot goes with her.' Georgie shook her hair back again, and stroked the pleats in her skirt so that it sat nicely. 'I could watch them, and then if she starts to go back to her room, I can run ahead and warn you.'

'You promise you can keep out of sight?' Henrietta scratched demandingly at Georgie's boots.

'I promise,' Georgie agreed, tucking her feet under the chair. She swallowed hard. 'We'll do it tomorrow.'

SIX

'There! She's gone off to the promenade deck.' Lily craned her neck around the corner of the passage.

'We'll follow her then,' Georgie said, her voice rather small. 'Ugh. Did you have to make this hat so big, Lily? It looks like I've got a cake on my head.'

They had decided earlier on that morning that Georgie had better be glamoured as well, just in case Mama spotted her. She was now several years older, and dressed in the height of fashion – Lily had copied the outfit from a colour plate in the *Ladies' Monthly Museum*, which someone had left lying around in one of the saloons.

'It isn't as big as the one in the picture!' Lily protested. 'I thought you'd probably fall over if I made it that huge. And it doesn't really look like a cake. More like a meringue.' She giggled.

'I don't know what you're complaining about,' Henrietta muttered. 'We need to go now, Lily. The sooner I'm out of this unnatural shape, the better.' She fluttered and shuddered, shaking out the green feathers irritably.

'If anyone comes, then I've the perfect excuse for being in her stateroom,' Lily said, for at least the sixth time. 'Everyone on board knows about that awful parrot. I'll just say that I found it flying about in one of the parlours, and brought it back.' She grinned at Henrietta. 'But you'll need to squawk, you know. It's always making the most unholy noise.'

Henrietta snarled, which was a rather strange sound, coming from a parrot. Lily was surprised she could still do it, actually, with a beak, but then she supposed the beak was only imaginary. The glamours she made weren't even as much as skin deep, since she'd never been taught the proper way to do them. If anyone stroked Henrietta, they would probably still feel fur. But then no one would be stupid enough to stroke Mrs Archibald's parrot, which was known to be vicious as well as noisy. And even if Henrietta's glamour was only thin, Lily was still very proud of it. She had glamoured herself and Georgie before, into old ladies, to disguise themselves in London, but she had never tried to glamour another creature. The spell had taken a while, and Henrietta had been forced to sit motionless and watch herself growing feathers. She was still in the worst of tempers.

'We'll see you soon,' Georgie told her. 'Be careful. And quick! Just a few minutes, remember? We don't know how long she'll be up on deck.'

Lily nodded, and watched them hurry away down the corridor.

'Why did your mother have to make her new spell-creature a parrot?' Henrietta growled. 'I hope you're not expecting me to fly, Lily. I've still got paws under all this, you know. It won't work.'

'Just flap a bit,' Lily told her consolingly. 'If anyone comes you could try fluttering around. There isn't a lot of space for proper flying in these passageways anyway.'

'A wolfhound. Would it really have made much difference?' Henrietta spat, making a series of ungainly hops to jump onto Lily's outstretched arm. 'You look perfectly normal. You're doing this to tease me.'

'The maid who does her room *is* perfectly normal!' Lily protested. 'I just had to make myself a little older and darken my hair. With the uniform on, everyone will just assume I'm a maid. It won't fool any of the staff who know the girl well, though.' She stopped in front of a smart white and gilt door. 'This is her room. She must have got some money from somewhere; this is one of the really expensive suites, I think.'

Henrietta fluttered down from her wrist and scrabbled awkwardly at the door handle. 'Ugh! These claw things are no good at all! And as I thought, Lily, this door is locked. Now what do we do?' Lily stroked her fingers lightly down the white wooden panelling, trying to feel for a spell. She didn't want to set off some sort of magical alarm and bring her mother hurrying back down from the deck. 'It's all right, I brought a spell with me to help. I found the idea for this in one of Daniel's books back at the theatre.' She drew a little cloth bundle out of her pocket, and unwrapped it.

Henrietta clawed her way up Lily's uniform sleeve to her shoulder, and peered down. 'Uuuugh, what is that?'

Lily eyed the contents of her parcel, wrinkling her nose. 'It's got a bit squashed. It's a spider, a very dead one, don't worry. I found it in the orchestra pit and I thought it might be useful. Spiders seem to come into quite a lot of the traditional sorts of spells. I think that's another reason Georgie never enjoyed her magic much.'

Henrietta leaned closer and shuddered. 'Wrap it up, Lily, please! I can't help myself, in this shape, it looks so succulent and leggy, I just want to eat it!'

Lily whipped the spider behind her back. 'You mustn't. We have to use one of the legs to pick the lock.'

Henrietta squawked derisively, and looked almost surprised at herself. 'We'd better hurry up, I'm starting to sound like a real parrot. I don't believe you can pick a lock with a dead spider, Lily. Daniel's book was having you on. Or it was just one of those misguided books full of silly myths about magic.'

'The spell sounded real to me. I've tied red cotton in and out of all the legs, like it said, and it's a nice long-legged one, the book said that was important. Now we're supposed to poke it into the lock, and pull the thread out again.' She eyed the parcel unwillingly – she had worn gloves (Georgie's: she hadn't told her) to wrap the thread around the spider, and she didn't really want to touch it now, with her bare fingers. Gingerly, she picked it out of the cloth, flinching at the slight furriness of its body and the shiny hardness of the legs.

'Hurry, Lily, I want to snap it up,' Henrietta moaned.

Lily closed her eyes and shoved, remembering to keep hold of the end of the thread. There was a most unpleasant squishing sensation, and she tugged convulsively on the thread, remembering at the last moment to mutter, 'Weaver of tiny miracles, slip this knot and open for me…'

The lock gave a satisfying clunk, and Lily tried the handle and pushed the door open. She whisked inside, closing it quietly behind her, and looked around.

The suite was prettily, fussily decorated, all gold and white like the door. It didn't seem right for Lily's mother at all. Lily always thought of her in dark places, like the library back at Merrythought. 'When we found that list of spells that she'd taught Georgie, the one that set us off thinking about the plot, it was in her photo album,' she murmured to Henrietta. 'Do you think she still has it? That little green leather book?'

'I remember.' Henrietta jumped down from her arm onto the bed, waddling up the silken coverlet and cursing squawkily as her claws caught in the slippery fabric. 'Not by the side of her bed, or under the pillows.'

'Look!' Lily hurried across the room to a small leather trunk banded in brass, like some sort of pharmacist's kit. It was full of little bottles with heavy glass stoppers, most of them filled with sludgy-looking liquids. And tucked down one side of the trunk was the green leather book.

'Be careful. She's not at home now – she might have set some sort of guard on it,' Henrietta snapped, as Lily crouched and reached out for the book.

'It looks just the same.' Lily longed to pick it up – she was suddenly sure that whatever they needed was inside, and she wanted it, so, so much. Her mouth watered, as though the little book was sugary sweet.

'Lily, stop it!' Henrietta flapped and skidded and

landed on top of the trunk with a ringing of little glass bottles. She snapped her beak at Lily's fingertips. 'You see, there's something burning these glamoured feathers,' she added, jumping to the floor, and fluttering about like a green and grumpy feather duster. 'We can't touch the book until we've taken it off. Ow.'

Lily wriggled back, stroking Henrietta anxiously – some of her feathers were smoking, but the real fur under the glamour felt no different. 'What is it?'

'Some sort of spelled poison. It smells like mushrooms. I do like a nice mushroom,' Henrietta sighed. Then she shook herself, and made a spitting sort of noise. 'I do *not*! Horrid greyish things, and the most innocent-looking ones are always poisonous. Whatever this spell is, it's very good at making people want to pick it up. I call that just plain nasty.'

'It made you think of food too,' Lily said thoughtfully. 'I wanted it because it was sugary, and lovely, like a little pink cake.' She glanced over at the table by the bed, and smiled. 'I thought so. There's a biscuit barrel in our room too.' She went over to open it, and brought out a handful of sweet biscuits, glazed with sugar crystals. She stuffed one into her mouth, and then crushed another in her hand so that it was just a mess of sugary crumbs. 'You have this one,' she told Henrietta, feeding a third to the parrot, and then she crouched back down by the trunk. 'But keep it in your mouth, don't swallow it. It's to stop you wanting to pick up the book.'

'This is very unkind,' Henrietta muttered, crumbs leaking out of both sides of her beak.

'And it means you can't peck me when I do this,' Lily said, swiftly whipping out one of Henrietta's imaginary tail feathers.

'What did you do that for?' the parrot squawked, spitting crumbs.

'Oh dear, I was hoping you wouldn't feel it, since they were only glamour feathers…'

'It felt like you were pulling half my tail fur out!'

'I'm really sorry. But look, now we've got something we can touch the book with.' Lily dropped the handful of crumbs on top of the little book, and swept them over its surface with the feather, which sizzled into a haze of glittering, burnt-sugar-smelling sparks.

'The crumbs have gone,' Henrietta said, curiosity overcoming her fury about her tail.

'I think they've fed the spell, hopefully,' Lily muttered. 'It isn't making me want to pick it up any more – I mean, I do want to, but I'm not desperate… I don't think it's gone, it's just not hungry, for a minute or so…' She darted a hand out, seizing the book and closing her eyes hopefully.

She seemed still to have a hand when she opened them again a moment later.

Hurriedly, she flicked through the pages, flinching as she saw the solemn faces of her older sisters again. Tucked next to the photograph of Georgie as a baby was a folded paper, a list, in purplish spidery writing.

'Is it any use?'

'Addresses,' Lily said slowly. 'In New York, and some in other cities in America. Mortimer Jones. Isabella Fountain. Rose Fell! Look, an address for her, in New York!'

'Magicians she's hoping to bring into the plot, like we thought.' Henrietta nodded with satisfaction. 'Remember it, and then put the list back.'

'Shouldn't we get rid of it?' Lily glanced at her in surprise. 'To stop her finding them?'

'No! Of course not – then she'd know we were here! We've two more days shut up in a floating coffin with her, Lily, think! Put it back. And sweep up those crumbs.'

Lily slipped the list back into the book and closed the covers, shuddering at the hungry sucking sound they seemed to make. Then she dusted away the crumbs as carefully as she could, and they hurried out of the sweet-smelling room.

*

'Look at it!' Lily breathed. She had never seen such a magical-looking city. A huge greenish statue towered over them as the ship sailed slowly by. The massive figure was swathed in metal draperies, and it seemed to be hazed in a cloud of golden magic. The huge torch it held up in one hand burned with streaming blue and scarlet flames, obviously made by some sort of spell.

'Can you imagine anything like that at home?' Georgie said, staring. 'I knew magic was allowed here, but I didn't expect *this*. They actually like it…'

'It's so beautiful,' Lily whispered, staring at the tall building along the shoreline, lit up in the mist of the early evening.

'It is,' Colette agreed. 'But you need to go back to the cabin, girls. I'm really sorry,' she added, as Lily flinched at the thought of squashing back into the hidden compartment. 'They're going to come and take our baggage really soon, before we go through Customs. They need the trunks. I had to tell the steward I'd accidentally packed a necklace in the wrong one, and I needed to find it before we docked. He's given me a few minutes' grace. I hate having to make you leave all this.' She waved at the violet-streaked sky.

'It's all right,' Lily murmured, turning reluctantly away from the shimmering green-gold figure.

'I tipped the steward,' Colette said, hugging her.

'I told him a lot of my costumes were really fragile, so please could he take special care of the trunks.'

They hurried back down to the cabin, sneaking quickly in between the anxious-looking staff.

'Did you hear?' Henrietta hissed when they were safely inside Colette's cabin. 'Mrs Archibald is throwing a fit, saying that someone's been in her cabin.'

'I hope that maid doesn't get into trouble,' Lily said, feeling guilty. She hadn't even thought about it until now.

Colette shook her head. 'I doubt she will. They'll just assume she's in one of her fusses. Everyone thinks Mrs Archibald is mad.'

'They'd be right.' Georgie shivered. 'I hope she doesn't do anything stupid. Did you leave something behind, Lily?'

'No. But maybe she can tell that the spell's been disturbed. That would explain why she hasn't made a fuss until now – it was only when she went to look at that list for herself that she noticed. Maybe she was working out where to go first, when we land.'

Someone knocked on the door, and Lily flung her arms round Georgie, whispering, 'See you soon!' Then she hugged Henrietta, and climbed quickly inside the trunk, closing her eyes and breathing the faint jasmine scent of Colette that lingered on her clothes. She could hear Colette hastily stuffing the clothes back on top of her and apologising to the steward – it sounded as though she was tipping him again.

Then the trunk was being carried, and Lily fought against the panic beating in her chest. It was the darkness, mostly – that and having no idea where they were going. Or who was carrying her. She clenched her fists, wishing she could put them over her eyes for another layer to shut out the dark. But she couldn't move her arms. Gasping, she fought to turn her head a little, suddenly sure that there was no more air. The sweet jasmine scent was suffocating her now.

Lily, stop it.

Lily gulped, unsure for a moment who it was that was talking to her.

Georgie?

Stop panicking, it doesn't help.

I didn't know you could do that! What about the spells, are you safe? Be careful! Worrying about Georgie wakening the spells suddenly made breathing less of a terror.

I didn't know I could either. And it isn't using much magic. The trunks are right next to each other, I think. I probably can't do this from much further away.

It's very clever, Lily told her humbly. *Sorry. I hate being shut in. I never liked it in the act, but at least I knew it was only for a minute or so.*

Georgie seemed to laugh inside her head. *I know. It's quite nice being better than you at something.*

Funny. I always thought you were better at everything, when we were back at Merrythought.

She could feel Georgie's sigh. *I like things better now.*

'I'm sorry it's not very grand.' Colette looked around, her cheeks flushing pink. 'In fact, it's a horrible hole. But until I've definitely been engaged by the theatre, I don't really know what I can afford.'

'It's fine,' Lily said. She'd been going to say that the room was nice, but it so obviously wasn't that it would have sounded stupid. They were high up in a tall, rickety house, and every floor they had climbed through on the way had been festooned with washing that smelled of fish. Colette had let them out of the trunks once they were in the battered old cab that had brought them from the harbour, thankfully. She'd had to pay the driver an enormous sum to carry the trunks up as it was; he would have expired halfway up the stairs if the girls had still been hidden away inside. He had looked rather surprised when they'd all three got down from the cab, but Colette had looked meaningfully at the flask strapped onto his belt, and he'd just shaken his head wearily.

'And I did manage to tuck away some provisions – I'm too tired to try arguing with that landlady about supper.' Colette shuddered. 'It would almost certainly be fish, and I just don't fancy it.' She dug a parcel wrapped in napkins out of one of her bags. 'Some pastries, and I can't remember what's in them. Could be anything. Lucky dip.'

Henrietta pranced over eagerly. 'Jam. Prawn. Something in curry sauce. Whatever that one is, don't eat it, it smells disgusting. And the rest are cheese puffs.' She looked meltingly up at Colette. 'I adore cheese puffs.'

Colette laid a napkinful of cheese puffs in front of her, and collapsed wearily onto the creaky iron bedstead. 'I'm actually not hungry. I think it's being back on dry land – most of me seems still to be swaying.'

Lily and Georgie shared out the rest of the pastries, and then curled up next to Colette. The amazing adventure of their arrival seemed to have slipped away, and instead they were left with convincing a stranger to accompany them back to England: a stranger that they hadn't even found yet.

'It'll be all right,' Lily said in a small voice. She wanted someone to agree with her. She was used to being the one who made things work, but she didn't feel like that in this dingy, fish-smelling room, with people shouting on the floor below.

'It'll be better tomorrow,' Georgie told her, reaching

over to stroke her hand. 'It's late, that's all. Tomorrow we'll be able to see everything, and it'll be exciting again.'

'Do you promise?'

Lily felt Georgie hesitate, and then Georgie patted her hand firmly and Lily felt like a little sister again.

'Yes.'

'This is it.' Lily looked up at the smart brick building. 'Spring Street. Number 110.'

'What is *that*?' Georgie asked, peering up at the side wall of the building, which was on a corner.

Lily frowned. 'An advertisement, I think. For sauce? And pickles...' She giggled. 'Look at the bit in the middle, it's a enormous sparkly cucumber.'

Emblazoned on the wall was a huge green vegetable, glowing with a soft, delicious magic. Lily could feel her mouth watering as she stared at it.

'Do you think it's the same sort of spell that Mama used on the photograph album?' Georgie asked, scowling up at the glowing magic on the bricks. 'It's making me hungry. I don't think that ought to be allowed; it isn't fair, surely? Making people buy things with magic?'

Lily shrugged. 'I wonder how much the magician who did it got paid? I hope it was a lot. It works, doesn't it?'

'When I was living with your Aunt Arabel, there were things like this in London, very occasionally,' Henrietta said, sniffing hungrily at the bricks at the base of the wall. 'But not this big, not ever. Shop signs that moved, perhaps. But even that cost so much to have done, people often didn't think it was worth the money.'

'I suppose a great many magicians fled here from London,' Lily said, frowning. 'They needed work, and they must have worked for a lot less than they would at home. Maybe Rose Fell made this one, since she lives here?'

Henrietta sniffed again. 'Maybe. But I don't think she's the only magician in this building. Can't you feel it? It positively reeks of magic.' She shook her ears happily. 'It smells very good. It's seeped all through the walls.'

'We should go in,' Lily said, dragging her fingers away from the pinkish bricks. Henrietta was right – it wasn't just a firm compulsion to buy Anstruther's Sauce and Fine Chutneys that she could feel, there was a deeper magic underneath. It was deliciously intriguing, and it could feel her too; it was questing curiously around her fingers, trying to see who and what she was.

They walked round to the front of the building, and Lily submitted to Georgie straightening her hat and dusting her boots with a handkerchief. There wasn't a great deal she could do about their dresses. Maria and

Georgie had run them up in the theatre wardrobe, neat navy ones with a sailor-suit look, for the journey. But they'd only had room for what they were standing up in (or lying down in, really) when they were smuggled on board, and even the smartest dresses look grubby after six days' wear and prolonged squashing inside a trunk.

'You could glamour us a bit,' Georgie said hopefully. 'Just to make us look a little smarter, Lily – please?'

'I don't think that's a good idea…' Lily said slowly. 'It seems a bit rude, when we're going to see another magician. Besides, she'll be able to tell it isn't real, won't she? So there isn't much point.'

Georgie sighed and nodded, and they hurried under the smart awning over the front doors, stepping back in surprise as the doors swung open in front of them with a well-oiled wheeze.

'Magical doors?' Henrietta murmured, prancing in. 'Showing off, but I like it! Come on in out of the way, Lily, I want to do it again!'

'Ssshh!' Georgie muttered, seeing a smartly-dressed young man walking across the entrance hall towards them. 'Stop it, Henrietta, you're showing us up.'

'I am interested in the magic,' Henrietta said loftily, stalking towards the doors and then jumping back from them with a little mock growl, like any normal dog playing a game. But the doors remained resolutely closed.

Henrietta sniffed them thoughtfully. 'Clever. They must sense the intentions of the person approaching,' she murmured.

The young man was standing just behind them now, watching her and nodding. 'Ingenious, aren't they?' he said, lifting his hat and bowing slightly. 'No one can enter the building for dishonest purposes – well, not to steal, anyway. The spell doesn't go much beyond that, but it's a start. Good day to you.' And he strolled forwards, the doors swishing open in front of him.

'I do like this place,' Henrietta sighed. 'It's a pity we can't stay. But perhaps when we bring magic back to England we shall be able to have clever doors. Be sure to remember them, Lily.'

Lily nodded. She was already walking through the luxuriously decorated entrance hall towards the stairs, drawn upwards by some deep magic that seemed to be calling to her already. Henrietta skittered after her excitedly, eager to meet this powerful magician at last.

Lily trailed her fingers along the walls as she climbed the stairs, loving the touch of this magical building. It felt alive, like a huge creature. It knew they were climbing to its heart, and it was watching them interestedly, she was sure.

'Lily…'

'What is it?' Lily started, turning back to Georgie. She

had been so deeply wrapped in the glowing magic that she'd almost forgotten that her sister was following her up the stairs.

'There's something wrong. I don't know what it is, but the spells inside me are – are moving.' Georgie had her arms wrapped tightly around her chest, as though she was trying to hold something in. 'I think something's calling them.'

'The magic in the house?' Lily asked, frowning. She couldn't imagine how something that felt so gentle and essentially good under her fingers could be stirring up Mama's dark spells.

'No… I'm not sure…' Georgie gasped suddenly, and she sank down into a little huddle on the steps. 'Oh, it hurts!'

'It's Mama,' Lily said, staring at her. 'It has to be.'

'She's doing something? She's calling the spells?' Henrietta asked, nuzzling Georgie's hand affectionately. She and Georgie argued all the time, but Henrietta regarded Georgie as hers too.

Lily shook her head. 'No. She's here. Rose's address was on her list, remember. She got here first.'

'We should go,' Georgie whispered.

Lily looked at her worriedly. Her sister looked so pale, as though she was about to be sick.

'I don't want to go…' she said gently. 'Can we find

somewhere safe to hide you? Can you bear being close to her for a while?' Then she frowned. 'You got closer to her than this on the ship, Georgie. Why is she only hurting you now?'

Henrietta snorted. 'What do you think your mother is talking to Rose Fell about, Lily? She's right here, and she's thinking about Georgie, and the plot, and the magic she's sealed inside your sister. That's what's waking it up.'

'We can't let her persuade Rose into being part of the plot,' Lily said anxiously, glancing up the stairs.

Georgie shook her head. 'No, you have to go. What's that little door on the landing up there?'

Lily hurried up and opened it. 'It's a broom cupboard, Georgie, you don't want to be stuck in there with all the mops!'

Georgie tried to straighten up, her hand on Henrietta's head, and the little dog pushed up, as though she could really lift Georgie to her feet.

'It doesn't matter, I'm coming with you,' she whispered. 'I don't want you going up there on your own. It's better now; I'm getting used to it.'

Lily hauled her up and gazed at her doubtfully. 'Do you really think you can?'

'Yes. If she's up there with this Rose Fell, I want to hear what she's saying.'

Lily blinked. 'But – we can't let her see us, Georgie. Do you mean sneak into Rose's rooms?'

'Yes. I know Princess Jane trusts her, but it's a long time since they knew each other. I want to see what she thinks of Mama. Then we'll know if we can trust her, won't we?'

'I suppose so,' Lily murmured, looking up the stairs again. She had been worrying about this morning – it was so important that Rose Fell should agree to help them. But now a tricky social call had turned into something entirely different. She took Georgie's hand and led her slowly up the stairs, examining the little name cards set into brass holders on the doors.

'This is her,' she whispered at last, looking at the curly emerald-green writing. 'What do we do now?'

'You haven't any more spiders on you?' Henrietta grunted.

'It's not locked.' Georgie was leaning wearily against the doorframe, her fingers wrapped round the handle. 'I could turn it and walk in.'

'Don't!' Henrietta snapped. 'I will, I'm smaller. I can at least see if there's somewhere we can hide and listen to what they're saying.'

Georgie turned the handle, her damp fingers slipping, and Henrietta pushed the door open a crack and wormed her way through, leaving the girls waiting outside. Lily's heart thudded painfully as she tried to listen for Henrietta. Time seemed to stretch out as she stood flattened against the wall of the landing, her hand tightly gripping Georgie's.

At last there came a delicate pattering of claws, and Henrietta slipped back through the gap. 'They're in a room at the far end of the inner passageway, talking, and there's a coat cupboard we could hide in.' She shook herself disgustedly, dislodging a shining white hair. 'There's also a cat, but then there's no accounting for taste.' She looked up at Lily and Georgie, and nudged the door further open. 'Come on.'

They crept in, blinking in the sudden light after the darkness of the hallway. The apartment was panelled in a pale, greyish wood, and smelled pleasantly of spices and sweet vanilla. Sunlight poured through from the room at the end of the passage, and Lily could hear voices – her mother's low, hoarse murmur, which made her shiver, and another voice, higher and older-sounding.

'I do see what you mean. Queen Sophia seems to have become quite unreasonable, and her mother always was. But I'm not quite sure what it is you're trying to do.'

Henrietta jerked her head and hurried to a small

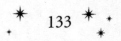

door, hustling them inside the coat cupboard and pulling on the hem of Georgie's skirt with her teeth to make her sit on the floor. 'Before you fall down,' she hissed.

Lily crouched down next to her, listening at the door, which they'd left cracked open.

'We want to bring the magic back,' she heard her mother say simply. 'That's all. It's been banned for so long now, and the country is suffering; you do see that, don't you?'

'But with the queen so opposed, how on earth are you going to… Oh. I see.'

'I'm so glad. It really is the only way, don't you think?'

'I suppose so…' It was merely a whisper, as though the old magician didn't want to agree. But she was! Their mother was persuading her!

Lily strained her ears to catch the conversation in the sunlit yellow room, but they'd lowered their voices too much, now that they were talking treason. It was impossible to hear until she stretched her fingers out of the crack in the doorway, curling them towards and beckoning the sound in with a dollop of her magic.

'We do have – well, one might call it a secret weapon.' Lily's mother's voice suddenly filled the tiny closet, husky and excited, and Georgie jammed her fingers into her mouth to stop herself crying out.

'Really…' Rose Fell sounded intrigued, worried…

And the voices weren't the only thing that came.

SEVEN

'Good morning.'

Lily had been crouching in the doorway, ignoring the ache in her knees, wanting to be as close to the voices as she could.

When the furry white face nosed itself around the edge of the door, she fell over backwards with a stifled yelp.

'What is it, Gus?' Rose called from the yellow room.

The cat stared at Lily and Henrietta, and their pleading eyes, and the pale huddled shape in the corner that was Georgie. 'A mouse,' he called back. Then he surged inside the cupboard and twitched his tail swiftly.

The door swung closed and the white cat began to glow, lighting up the dark and stuffy chamber.

'Well?'

'Oh please…' Georgie gasped.

'You mustn't let her…' Lily began at the same time.

'You first,' the cat said, dabbing Lily's hand with his damp nose. 'She looks like she's about to faint.'

'It's our mother doing that to her,' Lily explained hurriedly. 'I mean, that's our mother, talking to your – your –' She didn't like to say *mistress*, in case he was insulted.

'Companion. Go on.'

'She wants her to join in with a plot to overthrow the queen and bring back magic, and I know that doesn't sound like a terrible idea but they're doing it by filling their own children full of magic! Awful magic that's meant to kill people. Georgie's got the most horrible spells inside her, and she looks like that because the spells can feel Mama talking about them. Georgie is the secret weapon she just told you about.'

'She looks like butter wouldn't melt in her mouth,' the cat said disbelievingly, leaning forward to peer into Georgie's face.

'Of course she does, that's the point!' Lily hissed. 'If she looked like a murderous conspirator she wouldn't be much use, would she? She looks like a sweet little girl!'

'If she is sick in here, I will be most annoyed,' the cat

said, his whiskers twitching, as Georgie gagged, her shoulders shaking.

'I won't,' she gasped. 'It's just that she's still thinking about the magic. It wants to get to her.'

The white cat got up and paced solemnly over to Georgie, but Henrietta darted across the two steps of floor first and crouched half on Georgie's lap, poised to growl.

'I'm not going to hurt her, you idiot dog,' the cat said scornfully.

'Your mistress is conspiring with the person who got her into this state!' Henrietta snapped. 'Right this minute!'

'I assure you she isn't,' the cat replied. 'A mouse? In my apartment? Do you think that's likely? We have no vermin in *this* building.' Here the cat looked Henrietta up and down rather nastily. 'Usually. She knows quite well something is going on, and that I don't want her guest knowing about it.' He leaned over and trailed his absurdly long white whiskers over Georgie's cheek, and she gasped again, but this time with surprise.

'What did you do?' A little colour flushed back into her cheeks as they watched.

'Never you mind. I'm not having you making a mess; I am very sensitive to smell. Now stay here and behave yourselves while I go and talk to her.'

'You won't tell…' Lily began, but the cat sighed irritably.

'Be quiet, can't you? I'm about to open the door. And no, I won't. She needs cheering up. Two children and an unkempt dog in the hall cupboard might just do it.'

'You can come out now.'

The door swung open, and the girls blinked and clutched at each other in the sudden rush of light. Lily hadn't wanted to light up the darkness in the cupboard before, in case their mother saw it as she went past.

'Your mama seems quite annoyed with me,' the old lady standing behind the white cat said, smiling at them.

'You told her no?' Lily asked, trying to stand up and wobbling. Her feet had gone to sleep.

'I told her I would think about it,' the old lady said. She looked even older when she stopped smiling: she was very thin, and there were heavy dark shadows under her eyes. Lily could see why the white cat thought she might need cheering up. 'She wanted me to agree to return to London with her and join in this absurd-sounding plot.'

'It doesn't sound absurd when you've been dragged into it,' Lily said bitterly. 'We never wanted to be. Ask your cat what it's doing to Georgie.'

'Magical families do seem to trap people in the

strangest ways…' Rose said, staring at her. She turned abruptly. 'Come and sit down. There's tea, and cakes. Your mother didn't want any; you two look as though you could use them.'

Lily and Georgie followed her into the yellow-painted sitting room, with Henrietta pacing behind and scowling. When Rose sat down and the white cat leaped up to sit with her, Henrietta did the same to Lily, so she could glare at the superior creature from the same level.

Lily gave a little gasp of laughter as she thought that, remembering Princess Jane's description of the white cat she had once known. She had called him a most superior creature. Surely this had to be the same cat?

'What is it?' he snapped, his whiskers bristling.

'I'm sorry! It's just that we met someone who knew you, a long time ago, and – and I just realised that it was you she meant,' she ended tactfully.

'Who?' Rose asked curiously.

'The princess. Princess Jane,' Lily began to explain, but then she realised that everyone thought the princess was dead. 'Oh, except she wasn't sure if you would think she was dead. She said that you used to write to each other, a long time ago when you first came over here.'

'She *is* dead,' Rose said coldly. 'I saw the newspaper reports of the funeral. We're not completely backward here, you know.'

Lily ducked her head. 'It was a fake,' she murmured. 'They shut her up because she wouldn't denounce magic.' She glanced up to meet Rose's eyes again. 'It was mostly because of you that she wouldn't, so they hid her away. In your old house. They shut us up there too, and we found her.'

'In Fell Hall? They've turned Fell Hall into a prison?' Rose's face seemed to crumple. 'I'd heard rumours that there was a place for children now. I nearly went back, then, but I couldn't bring myself to see what they had done to our beautiful country. We concentrated on bringing people out, instead…' She shook her head. 'Jane is alive? Is she safe? What have you done with her?'

'She's hidden,' Henrietta said gruffly. 'And I don't think we ought to be telling you where, bearing in mind the company you keep.'

'Hen-ri-etta!' Georgie gasped, but Lily ran her hand down the pug's dense velvet fur, and stared back at Rose.

'I suppose you didn't know who she was, when she came calling.'

'I knew the name,' Rose admitted. 'And I had a suspicion of what she might want. It was obvious from the way she looked at me, even before she started to explain. Her eyes are hungry.'

Lily nodded. 'Would you have agreed to what she wanted, if your cat hadn't found us?'

Rose sighed, glancing over at a little table by her armchair with a framed portrait photograph on it. The photograph showed a large man, with luxuriant side whiskers and a collar that looked too tight for him. The cat nudged her lovingly, and she turned back to stare at Lily.

'No. I haven't really the energy for plots and intrigues. But I knew her mother – your grandmother. It would have been rude not to receive Amelia's daughter.' She frowned. 'Your mother isn't much like her. Though you do resemble her a little,' she told Georgie.

Lily looked down at Henrietta. She trusted the pug's nose more than a forty-year-old friendship with Jane.

Henrietta sniffed grumpily. 'She's probably all right,' she muttered. 'Though if she won't intrigue for your mama, she isn't going to do it for us either, is she?'

Lily was about to shush her when she caught the deep blue and orange gaze of the cat, staring at her across the room. He looked hopeful, she thought, almost pleading. As though he was willing her not to give up.

'What is Fell Hall like now?' Rose asked wistfully. 'I haven't seen it in so long.'

Lily exchanged a worried glance with Georgie. Was this a good time to admit that when they'd left Fell Hall, the ancient house had been collapsing into a pile of white stone as the dragons erupted from the underground caves?

'It was quite neglected,' she began slowly. 'They'd taken all the nicest furniture and sold it, I think. And the books and pictures.'

'I'd never been anywhere like it,' Rose murmured. 'I was brought up in an orphanage, did you know that?'

'I think the princess did say that you were an orphan,' Lily said slowly. 'But I thought that meant you didn't have any parents, not that you were actually in an orphanage.'

'I went to work for Aloysius Fountain as a maid, and spent weeks trying to work out why his house was talking to me.' Rose laughed. 'I really didn't understand. I knew nothing about magic, and I didn't like it. And then he took me on as an apprentice, when it became obvious the magic wasn't something I could get rid of.'

'Why would you want to be rid of it?' Lily asked, glancing at Georgie, who was staring at her feet.

'I had my first job, Lily! I'm sorry, but you can't understand what that was like for a child who'd always been living off charity. I understood how to be a housemaid. It was the sort of thing we were trained for at the orphanage. As I saw it then, the magic was ruining my only chance. But then I learned to love it, and eventually I discovered that I was a Fell and that magic was part of my family. For someone who had never had a family at all, that made the magic even more special.' She smiled, gazing across the room at nothing. 'That house. It was even more beautiful than the palace, I thought. I suppose I should have realised they'd take the paintings… I used to spend so long looking at them, trying to see my own face, the colour of my hair… It was wonderful.'

'It fell down,' Lily muttered, feeling that she couldn't bear to hide the truth any longer.

Gus's tail twitched back and forth, but Rose was still.

'We found – I found – well, we didn't really mean to, and I don't think it was just us, it was all the magic that wasn't being used because we weren't allowed. Although he did say it was because I had Fell blood in me too, so I suppose it was me a bit—'

Henrietta thwacked Lily's arm with her solid little tail. 'Shut up, Lily. You sound deranged. What she's trying to say is that she woke up a dragon, and then we rescued all the children, and Princess Jane. We flew out of Fell Hall on his back. Then a whole lot of his friends and relatives woke up, and flew out of the middle of the house, and it collapsed. There. Sorry.'

Rose went white, and Lily thought she was about to faint at the awfulness of the news, but instead she leaned forward excitedly. 'You found them! You truly found the dragons?'

Lily nodded. 'Most of them went back to Derbyshire, to find some more caves to live in, I think. But the silver one, he was sort of their leader, and he decided to stay with us. He's at the theatre, in London, with our friends. He's pretending to be papier-mâché scenery. He quite likes it,' she assured Rose. 'He likes to watch the acts. He's a very good dance master, actually, the ballet dancers always do what they're told now.'

'We used to see them,' Rose murmured. 'Or we'd think we did. Just vanishing round corners in front of us. Or the stonework would twitch – there were all those carvings...'

Lily nodded. 'Yes. He was a carving. Part of the overmantel in one of the upstairs rooms, the bluish-silvery marble one. We talked to him, and then he talked back... He said that they were so much part of the house, they could use it to move around, even though really they were asleep in the caverns, deep under the foundations of the house.'

'There were stories about those caves,' Rose agreed. 'We went looking for them, Bill and Bella and Freddie and I, but we never found a way in. There were stories about the dragons, too. The silver one was the best known – his name is Argent.'

Lily nodded slowly. It sounded right for him, but she felt guilty. They had never asked his name. 'We didn't know that – somehow I didn't think of him having a name. He was just the dragon, the silver dragon.'

Rose smiled at her. 'Argent only means silver. I shouldn't think he minded. Oh, Argent!' She lay back in her chair, smiling, and then Lily noticed that tears were running down her face.

'What is it? We're really sorry about the house. We never knew that waking the dragons would do that, but we had to get away. I think we'd have done it even if we did know; I'm sorry. Fell Hall was an awful place, for us.'

'It isn't that. I never thought I'd go back there, anyway,' Rose gasped. She drew in a shuddering breath, trying to calm herself. 'I just wish Bill was still here. He never believed in them, never. He used to laugh at us, and he refused to see them in the passageways, even when the rest of us swore to him they were there. I'd just like to see his face, that's all.'

'When did he die?' Lily asked quietly.

'A month ago. His heart gave out – too much good living, but he was like me, he'd been deprived for so long before he went to live at the Fountain house. When he made his money, he couldn't help spending it.'

'He wasn't a magician?' Georgie asked, curiously.

Rose laughed. 'No. He thought it was all pretty nonsense, most of the time. He came out with us, though, when we had to leave, and I supported the pair of us when we were first married. He went to work on the docks, but he saved all his wages, and bought railroad stock. He said railroads were the future of America, and he made me invest too. And he was right. He was a millionaire,' she added proudly. 'A railroad tycoon, all from nothing.'

'If you came back with us, you could meet the dragon,' Lily said. She'd decided there was no point in dancing around it trying to be subtle. The white cat rolled his parti-coloured eyes at her in disgust, but Rose nodded slowly.

'I suppose… I'd never thought I would go back. We were treated so badly.'

'Not as badly as the magicians are being treated now,' Lily told her bluntly. 'I know you don't want to be plotting, and we hate what Mama is trying to do. We don't want anyone to hurt the queen. But it can't carry on like this, it just can't. Our father is shut away in a prison, and he isn't the only one. The Queen's Men are arresting everyone, and it's getting worse and worse. No one's been using magic in England for so long that it's all in the earth and the air, it wants to be used. That's what the dragon – Argent – told us. It keeps bubbling up in people when they don't expect it, and then they get into terrible trouble. We have to make Queen Sophia see that it's dangerous.'

Rose was frowning. 'Magic as a power stored in the land? I hadn't thought of it like that.'

'But do you see what it means? We have to get people using it again, lots of people. And not Mama's lot!' Lily jumped up and seized Rose's hands. 'We really need you to help. You told her about the spells inside Georgie, didn't you?' she asked the cat, and he nodded regally. 'The only person who we think can get rid of them is our father – he knows how Mama's magic works, you see, or at any rate we hope he does. But he's shut up in Archgate. You have to help us get him out, please! You helped to cast the spells for it, didn't you?'

Rose shuddered. 'I did, and I hated it. The old queen persuaded us, and it was after that madman had killed the king. It seemed reasonable that for criminal magicians one needed a magical prison. But it was a nightmare place. I still dream of it, even now.'

'And you were never shut in it,' Georgie said, looking up at last.

Rose blinked. 'No. I wasn't.' She stroked her hand down the white cat's back, from ears to tail-tip, and to Lily it seemed that they were deciding together, without words. Then she lifted her hand from his fur, and nodded. 'Yes. Gus and I will come. I will go and book our passage this afternoon.'

Lily flushed pink, and looked anxiously at Georgie.

'I'm afraid we don't have very much money. We borrowed a little from our friend Daniel, who owns the theatre, but we haven't enough for the ship. We stowed away to get here...'

Rose smiled. 'But I do have quite a lot. And I actually own a considerable share of the shipping company, so it isn't as if I'm really going to pay anyway.'

'Lily, wake up!'

Lily turned over, moaning in her sleep, and tried to ignore Henrietta, who was pushing a cold nose into her ear.

'Wake up, I tell you! Lily, now!'

'What! It isn't morning, and I've only just got to sleep.'

'You shouldn't have been gallivanting about so late, then,' Henrietta snapped.

Lily sighed and sat up. It was rather nice being on board a ship when one had a ticket paid for, and was a guest of a member of the board. There had been time for a quick but grateful goodbye to Colette, who was jittering about an audition at a well-known theatre, and for Georgie to run out and spend the money that Rose had pressed into her hands on new dresses for both of them, too. Even Lily, who didn't usually care about dresses, had to admit that it was nice not to be wearing navy any more.

'Something's happening,' Henrietta growled. 'I felt it. The ship *shook*! I don't like it. Lily, you need to get up, and we'll go and see.'

But Lily shook her head slowly. 'No. We don't need to. I know what it is.'

'An iceberg?' Henrietta darted to the end of the bed, trying to look out of the porthole. 'I knew all that boasting about these ships being unsinkable was nonsense.'

Lily smiled. 'It's him.'

EIGHT

'He's here?' Rose stared at Lily, her eyes wide and glowing with excitement. She was wearing a pretty ruffled nightgown, and her long silver hair trailed down her back in a plait. For a moment, Lily thought she looked no older than Georgie.

'He's twisted in between the funnels. It was the only place he could fit. He wants to see you – he says you called him by his name, and so he's come. I think he wants to fly us back home!'

'Let me get dressed. I'll write a note to the steward, explaining we were called away – they'll enjoy trying to work out what that means, I'm sure.'

Gus prowled to the end of the bed, his whiskers twitching slightly. 'Do I understand that we are going –

flying?' he asked faintly.

'It isn't as bad as you might think,' Henrietta told him airily. 'Of course, cats are sensitive,' she added, in a sweet growl.

'I suppose this dragon is very large,' Gus said gloomily, leaping down from the bed and stalking past Henrietta as if she didn't exist. She watched him affrontedly, and Lily sighed. Henrietta hated it when people ignored her. It was going to be difficult if she and Gus couldn't get on. Lily had been surprised when Rose called the white cat Gus, as it didn't seem a grand enough name for such a gentleman of a cat. But Rose had explained that it was short for Gustavus, which was much more suitable, Lily thought. Rose had also told her that Gus was older than she was – he had been Mr Fountain's cat before he adopted her, and he was at least seventy.

They hurried up to the main deck, keeping to the shadows and looking out for members of the crew. It would be easier not to have to explain why they were out at four o'clock in the morning.

'Hello!' Lily whispered excitedly, pattering along the deck and waving to the dragon, who was stretching his long neck down to look for them. 'I'm back, I've brought her!'

The dragon's eyes seemed to glow in the dim light

from the bulbs strung along the deck, and he half opened his wings, flapping them a little as though he wanted to fly, a victory flight out over the sea. 'Miss Fell?' he whispered, and his whisper made the boards of the deck shake under Lily's feet. 'I am Argent. You called to me.'

Rose half curtseyed to him, very gracefully, Lily thought. But then she had been used to being around princesses, and had probably had a lot of practice.

'Mrs Sands, actually,' she said to the dragon. 'I got married.'

The dragon snorted. 'You are still a Fell, whatever you call yourself. Dear Lily and Georgiana have a hint of the bloodline, enough to draw me out of my enchanted sleep, but you! A direct descendant, even if not bred at the Hall.' His head weaved around her as though he was drinking her in. 'It gives me strength even to look at you.' He flexed his massive claws, scraping them along the metal roof with an eerie shriek. 'Why are you on this – this smoky metal lump? Are you coming back to London? I will fly you – you can't crawl over the sea like this.'

'Must we really?' Gus muttered. 'I don't mind the smoke…'

'You have a familiar?' the dragon asked curiously, leaning further down, so that he was nose to nose with Gus. The white cat sat frozen on the deck, his whiskers sticking out dead straight and his eyes slits, as the dragon's hot breath swirled around him.

'She does,' he hissed defiantly, his ears almost flat against his skull.

'Good.' The dragon extended one fearsomely-taloned foot, clearly inviting Gus to climb into it. 'A Fell child should not be lonely. May I ask your name, dear cat?'

'Gustavus.' Gus glanced unhappily at Rose, and then stalked forward, climbing onto the dragon's foot as though he suspected it might be the last thing he ever did.

The dragon lifted Gus delicately to his back, placing the cat high up between his wings with a ceremonial flourish. 'Sit there, where you can see. Are you quite comfortable?'

Gus looked tiny on the back of such a huge creature. He peered down at them, his eyes round with relieved surprise. 'Oh, indeed...' he muttered.

'Miss Rose.' The dragon stretched out his foot again, depositing the white-haired lady carefully behind her cat. Rose stroked Gus gently, and the cat hunched his shoulders, as if he didn't much care for petting. But the panicked glitter went out of his eyes, and he edged backwards a little along the dragon's spine so that he was nestled into her skirts.

Lily picked up Henrietta, who was looking slightly

sulky at all this attention being paid to Gus, and she and Georgie climbed up behind.

'Hold tight,' the dragon cried joyfully, and he leaped out over the row of lifeboats, setting them swinging with the draught of his wings as he shot out over the black sea.

Lily heard a strangled sort of mew from Gus, and Henrietta hunkered down between her knees, growling softly.

As they swooped down towards the dark water, Argent opened his wings out fully and began the strong steady beat that Lily was used to. 'Sorry,' he called back over his shoulder, the words floating past Lily on the whistling wind. 'No room to stretch out back there on that poky little boat.'

Lily gazed down at the waves rolling below them, their white crests shining in the faint moonlight. They seemed to be flying incredibly fast – much faster than they had on their flight from Fell Hall.

'Argent…' It seemed odd to call him by his name, almost rude, when he'd never told it to her, but he glanced around as he heard her calling. 'We're going so fast!'

'I'm stronger now,' he told her simply. 'Carrying a Fell, you see. My magic is growing back stronger than ever; can't you see it, dearest Lily? Watch my wings!'

Lily and the others peered sideways, clinging tightly to the spikes along his back. 'Oh! It isn't moonlight!' Georgie gasped. 'It's you!'

'If anyone sees us, they'll think you're riding on a shooting star,' the dragon said rather smugly, flourishing his glowing wings so that a wash of light scattered off them like sparks falling to the water below.

'Can you turn it off again?' Lily asked anxiously. 'No one at the theatre will be able to believe you're made of papier-mâché if you glow. You'd cost a fortune in that smart luminescent paint, the size you are.'

'I can…' the dragon muttered. 'If I must. Do you not like it?' he added, rather plaintively.

'It's beautiful,' Lily said quickly, patting his huge side. 'So clever. Just very shiny. You're right, you'll be confusing sailors all over the place.'

'We should be back in London before the night is out,' he called back, his deep voice ringing triumphantly.

'You can't possibly!' Rose exclaimed. 'It's five days' journey, at least!'

'Not for a dragon. We'll race the sun,' he roared, beating his wings faster and faster so that they settled into a shining blur.

'Well, I hope he knows where he's going,' Henrietta muttered, huddling herself under Lily's cloak. 'Wake me when we get home.'

'This is Daniel,' Lily explained, wishing that he hadn't dressed quite so fast. She had wanted him to make a good impression, and he looked wild-eyed, his hair sticking up in mad curls. 'He owns the theatre, and he rescued us, when we first came to London and we had nowhere to stay.'

Daniel bowed clumsily and stared at Rose, quite tongue-tied. Lily realised that she probably featured in several of his books about magic, and he was starstruck.

'Rose!' The princess hurried eagerly down the passageway and dashed into the yard. She was carrying an armful of gauzy net and had obviously been sewing something for Maria, but she flung the costume into Lily's arms and ran towards her old friend. 'I didn't think I'd ever see you again,' she said tearfully, holding her at arm's length and gazing at her. 'You look so much the same. And darling Gus. I think I have, yes...' She searched in the hanging pocket of her dress. 'Do you still like violet comfits? One of the stagehands knew a little place where one could still get them, though they're very old-fashioned now.'

Gus's ears twitched, and he accepted the sweet delicately and then prowled round behind Rose to spit it out. He glanced up at Lily as though daring her to comment, but she quickly squashed it to a sugary powder with her boot and he nudged her gratefully.

'Has anything else happened while we've been away?' Lily asked Daniel, leaving the old friends talking. 'Daniel, stop staring at her!'

'Sorry! Ummm, not a great deal. More of the same, I suppose. Another attack of magic in the audience last night. They're starting to mention it in the newspapers now; the Queen's Men can't suppress the stories any more. Will she be staying here?' he added eagerly.

'Oh! I haven't asked. She's ever so rich, apparently, she could rent apartments somewhere, if she wanted, or go to a hotel. But I should think she'd like to be here with the princess and the dragon. She can hardly take him to the Savoy, can she?' Lily glanced sadly at the dragon – it wasn't as if such a creature could really belong to anyone. But if he did, she had a feeling he was Rose's now.

What happened to him anyway? Peter held up his notebook with the scribbled question, and Daniel nodded.

'He launched himself out of here like there was a fire, about three days ago. Not a word! Lucky it wasn't the middle of a performance; I shouldn't think he'd have cared if it was.'

'She called him,' Lily sighed. 'She knew his name, you see. He's called Argent, he's a family legend. And his magic's woken up even more now that he's found her.'

The dragon, who had been purring happily to himself as the sun rose higher and warmed a little more of the yard, and him, snaked his tail closer to Lily, Daniel and Peter. He coiled the silvery mass around Lily's legs, making her squeak, and drew her closer to him. 'She may have strengthened me, little one, but you woke me first. I shall never forget that. And I shan't forget our mission, either, to rescue your sister. Those spells are growing stronger inside her – I can feel the difference in her after only a few days apart.'

'We saw our mother in New York,' Lily muttered anxiously, her worry about Georgie fighting with happiness that the dragon still cared about her. 'I think being close to Mama made Georgie worse. She said the spells hurt her.'

'We should go and look at the prison.' Rose and the princess were standing behind Lily, looking serious. 'I don't know if they've changed any of the spells we set up, but I may be able to tell if I'm close.'

'We could pretend to be sightseers looking at the palace,' Lily suggested.

'I could go with you, if I were veiled, perhaps?' Princess Jane suggested. 'I know I look like Sophia, but with a thickly veiled bonnet, surely it would be safe enough? Then I could show you what I remember of the key spell.'

'That would help,' Rose agreed.

'The sooner we do this, the better,' the dragon told them, his massive tail swishing across the stage so that Henrietta had to scuttle out of its way. 'Now that I'm back, I can feel that fallow magic I told you of before, Lily. It's starting to be shaped... I can't quite tell what's doing it. Some huge magical working, that's all I can sense. That, and I don't like it.'

Lily stared at him. 'It can't be the plot against the queen, can it? Mama is still in New York!'

'But all the others aren't. Jonathan Dysart's here, and those sly daughters of his.' Henrietta scratched at Lily's knees to be picked up. 'We always thought they were part of it, after what they said to you. They're setting it going. Everything points to it.' She gazed thoughtfully at Georgie's white, anxious face. 'They're getting the plot under way already.'

'It doesn't look like a magical door.' Lily tried to hold her little red-bound copy of Mrs Satterthwaite's *Guide to the Metropolis* in an obvious position. They hadn't known quite what else to do to make themselves look like sightseers. Daniel had snorted when they asked him, and said just to stand in everybody's way as much as possible, and try to make stupid comments about all the monuments.

'It isn't supposed to, idiot child,' came an acid whisper from Rose's large basket. It was supposed to look like a picnic lunch, and Gus had tried to suggest that perhaps there should be food in it just in case anyone checked. He had particularly recommended salmon sandwiches, or even fish paste, in a pinch, but Rose had told him there wasn't time. 'Hold it up a bit, I can't see! This is so undignified.'

Henrietta sniggered and, for once, didn't complain about wearing a lead.

'Does it look the same as it did before?' Lily asked Rose and the princess. She scuffed her boot gently over the paving slabs. Her father was under here somewhere. It was hard to imagine.

'I wish we could get closer,' Rose murmured. 'It's hard to tell. I can feel the spells – my spells. They call to me. But there may be other magic around them that I don't recognise.'

'My whiskers aren't itching,' the voice from the basket commented. 'It all feels like familiar magic to me – apart from the key spell, which is simply archaic. Effective, though, unless of course you happen to have a stray princess lying around.'

Gus's tone suggested that he was trying to be rude, but Princess Jane wasn't listening. 'Those girls over there are staring at you,' she commented, eyeing two smartly-dressed girls who were walking towards them from the palace mews.

Lily glanced round. 'Oh, no…' she muttered. 'They must have been visiting their father. Or else he's already got them dancing attendance on the queen, as part of the plot.'

'Who are they?' Rose murmured. 'They feel familiar.'

'They've probably been filled with the same poisonous spells as Georgie,' Lily sighed. 'Their names are Cora and Penelope Dysart, and their father is a counsellor to the queen. He's always making speeches to the newspapers about how awful magic is, but he's a magician himself.'

'Ohhh…' Georgie moaned suddenly, doubling over. 'I can't stop them!'

'What is it?' Lily asked anxiously, one eye on Georgie and the other on Cora and Penelope, who were coming ever closer, holding matching parasols.

'Don't let them get close,' Georgie whispered, collapsing to the pavement.

A few passers-by stopped, and Rose crouched beside Georgie, holding her head and fanning her gently. 'Please don't worry. Just the heat. She's rather sensitive to the sun, poor child.'

'Get away,' Georgie moaned. 'Get away, it isn't safe…'

Rose sat back in surprise as Georgie's words died out, the whispers spiralling into a greenish-grey vapour that was stealing from her mouth.

'What is that?' someone muttered behind them. 'Look at her!'

Lily saw the Dysart girls turn and hurry quickly away. One of them – she couldn't be sure which – cast a triumphant smile at Lily over her shoulder.

'They did it,' she muttered. 'It was their spells, calling to Georgie's somehow. We have to get her back to the theatre.'

'I don't think we can move her now,' Princess Jane said quietly.

The greenish smoke was pouring out of Georgie's mouth – no one was going to believe that she had only fainted from the heat now.

'We have to!' Lily hissed. 'Someone's probably gone looking for the Queen's Men already. We're right outside the palace, we have to—'

'Lily, be quiet! What is that green stuff?' Henrietta muttered, hoping that no one was looking at her. 'What is it doing?'

Lily stopped. She had been thinking about getting Georgie somewhere safe, but Henrietta was right. She crouched down next to Rose, watching the spell swirling around her sister. She remembered the dusty wolf that

Georgie had accidentally created to fight Marten, and hoped that this strange smoke wasn't as dangerous.

'Do you know what the spell is?' she whispered to Rose.

'It isn't something I've ever cast myself, but I think it's a binding spell. It shouldn't be green like this – we shouldn't be able to see it at all. Your sister's fighting it, I think, as well as she can; she's added the colour. It's supposed to trap someone so they can't move. Stay back.'

'Can you get rid of it?'

'Not without making it obvious that I'm a magician too. I think if we stayed away from her it would just seep away eventually. But we don't have that much time.' Rose looked around anxiously. 'Here they come.'

A column of men in dark uniforms was striding towards them from the palace, and the crowd of bystanders shifted restlessly. Lily heard a few hisses.

'We need to get away! They'll take her. We can't let them.'

'This spell – you can take it off?' Henrietta muttered to Rose. 'In private?'

Rose nodded. 'I think so.'

'Then be ready, Lily. Run fast.' Henrietta darted away from them, scuttling into the green smoke with her head down and clawing at Georgie's arm. Lily saw Georgie begin to shift, and lift her head wearily, and then the cloud of smoke swirled and thickened and darkened. It sealed itself around the little black dog, and Georgie screamed, 'Henrietta, no!'

But the smoke had gone, and Henrietta lay limply on her side.

And as far as Lily could tell, she was dead.

Georgie seized the faded bundle of black fur, and Lily ran to help her up. 'We have to run, she said to run!' she told Georgie. 'Come on!'

'You get them away,' an old man muttered to her. 'No one's going to tell them where you went. Hurry now!'

Lily nodded to him. She seized Henrietta from Georgie, who could hardly stand up, grabbed her sister's hand and dragged her away. Rose and the princess followed, and they hurried down the wide road, watching the crowd knit themselves together in front of the advancing men.

'Through the park,' Rose muttered, panting. 'They already know what we are now; I can hold them off there if they're chasing us. I don't want to hurt anybody.'

But the crowd seemed to have delayed the Queen's Men for long enough. There was no one following them as they headed back through the park, threading their way along quieter streets to the theatre.

As they hurried through the yard into the passageways under the theatre, Gus leaped out of the covered basket, swarming up Rose's arm to lean over and sniff at Henrietta's limp body.

'She shouldn't have done it,' he muttered. 'It was meant for a human – the queen, I suppose. Too much spell for someone so small.'

'You mean you can't wake her up?' Lily looked at Rose, her eyes widening in shock. 'No! You said you could!'

Rose sighed. 'I didn't realise what she was going to do.'

Lily hugged Henrietta close, missing her solid warmth, and tears ran down the side of her nose and splashed onto the dusty-looking fur. 'I didn't either. Bad dog...' she added, in a miserable whisper.

'What happened to her?' Sam gasped, walking out of the carpentry workshop with Peter following him and seeing Henrietta in Lily's arms. 'Did she get knocked down?'

'It's a spell,' Lily told him in a choked voice, letting him cradle the dog in his massive hands. 'She did it so we could escape – it was one of Georgie's, the bad ones.'

'I'm sorry!' Georgie cried. 'I didn't mean to!'

'Can't you take it off?' Sam demanded, staring at her.

Georgie started to shake her head, but Rose frowned.

'Perhaps she can. Here.' She hurried into the workshop. 'Lay her down.'

Sam swept the workbench clear of wood shavings with one sleeve, and laid Henrietta gently down.

Rose pulled Georgie forward. 'I know you don't think you can, but you changed that spell. My guess is that you were frightened it would hurt Lily, or us, and you were trying to protect us all. And if you can do that, if you've got enough control to alter the spells, then you can lift this if we help you.'

Georgie nodded doubtfully. She stood in front of the workbench, one hand held out, just touching Henrietta's fur. 'I can feel the spell on her,' she admitted. 'But it doesn't feel like part of me, like my magic ought to.'

'It came out of your mouth,' Lily said suddenly. 'Please, Georgie. It's Henrietta. *Please.*'

Georgie closed her eyes and laid her hand down flat on Henrietta's side. Then she pinched her fingertips together like someone picking up a thread, and pulled, winding something around the fingers of her other hand.

'What's she doing?' Sam whispered loudly.

'It's like a cocoon,' Georgie said, her voice echoing a little, as though it came from a long way away. 'A silk moth. All wrapped up inside.' She kept winding the thread of magic round her fingers, and the others could see it now, a fine, green thread, the coil growing thicker and thicker. 'You have to help me hold it,' she muttered at last. 'It's heavy.'

Lily reached out, cautiously picking at the bundle of poison-green magic round her sister's fingers. It stuck, and buzzed, and she could smell it now as well, metallic and nasty.

'What are we going to do with it?' she asked Rose, but the old magician was already holding out a little silken bag, woven with magic. Lily could see the spells glowing and pulsing along the woven fabric.

'We'll keep it,' Rose explained. 'No point in wasting a strong spell. It may not be something I'd want to cast myself, but it might be useful. Keep unwinding it. You –' she pointed to Peter – 'hold Georgie up. She's weakening. Georgie, be careful. Don't breathe it in, remember.'

Peter frowned and came to stand behind Georgie. She was still uncoiling the thread, but more slowly now, and her head was hanging. Georgie shifted wearily as Peter put his hands on her shoulders. 'I'm bringing her back, I promise,' she whispered.

'She moved!' Lily said suddenly, accidentally pulling on the green thread in her excitement.

Henrietta jerked, and growled faintly.

'Sorry, sorry! Henrietta, come on, wake up!'

'Not if you're going to pull my whiskers out like that,' the black pug answered, in a whisper.

'Can you move?' Rose asked, stuffing the last of the spell-thread into the bag.

Gus leaped onto the workbench, tickling his silver whiskers across Henrietta's fur. 'It's gone,' he reported. 'She's clean.'

Henrietta surged upright, the fur along her spine rising. 'Of course I'm clean,' she snapped. 'You – you cat!'

Lily picked her up, holding her so that the small black head tucked under her chin. She could feel how tired Henrietta was. 'You shouldn't have done that,' she said, trying to sound cross. 'What if we hadn't been able to get rid of the spell?'

'Well, we couldn't pick *you* up and run away, could we?' Henrietta yawned. 'And I didn't notice the cat volunteering. I am very tired now. I should like a sleep, in the middle of your bed, Lily. And when I wake up I will have a whole meat pie, from the man with the stall round the corner. Send Ned; he may as well make himself useful.'

NINE

'So you really think you can get us to him?' Lily whispered, digging her nails into her palms anxiously.

Rose nodded. 'I couldn't feel any magic that had been changed – not for the outer spells anyway,' she added warningly. 'I can't tell what's been done inside.'

'You should go soon,' the dragon rumbled. 'Before your sister's spells gather any more strength.'

Lily glanced over at Georgie, who was leaning back against the dragon's tail, huge dark shadows circling her eyes. 'Tonight?' she asked Rose hopefully. 'If you're strong enough, Princess,' she added, looking at Princess Jane, and Rose, and remembering how old they really were. But the princess didn't look as though she'd been running away from her sister's guards only that morning. Her eyes were bright blue and sparkling, and she was smiling and tickling Gus behind the ears, as though she wasn't a wanted fugitive at all.

'I think we should move quickly,' Rose agreed. 'As soon as it's fully dark.'

'Tonight. We'll have Father with us tonight, Georgie! We might even be able to start getting the spells off you tomorrow!' Lily told her gleefully.

'Don't be too hasty,' Gus purred. 'You don't know what it's like in there.'

Lily's smile faded. 'No. I suppose not. It's just that we've waited so long. I can't help being a little excited.'

'How do we get in? How does the key spell work?' the dragon asked curiously, staring down at Princess Jane.

Lily swallowed. 'I don't think… Argent, I'm sorry, but you're so big, people will see you. We have to sneak up to the prison.'

'But I want to be there to protect you!' The dragon reared his head up in surprise. 'Look what happened when you went out without me before!'

Gus climbed carefully up the dragon's tail, trotting along his back to the spot between his wings so he could talk to the enormous creature. 'Don't worry. This time I won't be hiding in a basket. I will make sure they don't do anything stupid.'

'So will I,' Henrietta put in swiftly. 'The cat as well.'

'Heroic isn't always helpful,' Gus hissed at her, his whiskers sparking crossly.

'Ssshh!' Rose sighed. 'Stop bickering. I wish we could prepare for this more. But Argent's right, at least we'd better make sure we understand how the key spell works.'

'It seemed quite simple the couple of times that I did it,' the princess said doubtfully. 'I just stood in front of the door – it's hidden, of course, but there's a particular figure in the carving to look for. She has a robe on, with a Greek key pattern around the edge, as a clue. All I had to do was take her hand, and then in her other hand she would hold out the key.'

'It's really that easy?' Lily said doubtfully. It seemed a little simple for something so important.

'It only works for a member of her family, Lily!' Georgie pointed out. 'It's one of the most secure spells there is!'

'Yes... I suppose they never thought one of the family might change sides. Sorry,' she added quickly. 'I didn't mean that to sound rude.'

The princess nodded. 'I know. But I don't think I have changed sides, Lily. The rest of my family changed, not me. I should have seen the way it was leading, when Archgate was built.'

Rose sighed. 'I should never have agreed to be part of it,' she said bitterly.

'Don't be stupid.' Gus stared down at her from the dragon's back. 'If you hadn't, we would have no chance of getting beyond the main door. Think of it as forward planning. We should have known we'd have to burgle the place one day.'

'That's the patrol going by,' Henrietta whispered in Lily's ear. 'We should go as soon as they round the corner of the wall.'

Lily watched as the detachment of black-uniformed men marched past, disappearing around the corner of the palace wall just beyond the archway. Then she stole out from behind the base of the statue they'd been lurking behind, beckoning the others after her. They were all wrapped in dark cloaks left over from a dancing-skeleton comedy act that had been part of the show years ago. Maria never threw anything away. They hurried into the shadowy arch, and Princess Jane stroked her fingers over the marble carvings.

'You can tell it's magical!' Lily murmured. 'It ought to be pitch-black in here, there's hardly any moon! And instead the marble's glowing, like that carved mantel at Fell Hall. Where's the figure; can you see it?'

Rose lifted Gus up next to the princess and Lily saw

that he was glowing too, his white fur shining softly like a lamp.

'Useful,' Henrietta muttered enviously, and Lily stroked her ears.

'Here!' The princess patted the hand of a tall woman, carved into the victory scene on the wall. She was supposed to be some sort of emblem of the royal bloodline, Lily guessed. She had a crown on, and a particularly foolish, smug sort of expression on her white stone face.

Lily traced a finger over the Greek key pattern – it had been added later than the rest of the carving, she could tell, for the lines of the pattern were still fresh and crisp. It made sense that it would have been added when the key spell was set. She watched curiously as Princess Jane slipped her own pale fingers in between the stone ones and squeezed, very gently.

There was a buzzing, creaking sound, like some long-unused machinery shifting into gear, and the princess gasped.

'Is it not working? Are you all right?' Rose asked anxiously.

'I think it is… But slowly. It doesn't know me, the spell, after so long… Be ready to take the key, someone – I can't move.' Jane had both her hands wrapped around the stone fingers now, and the carved face wasn't foolish any more. The eyes were sharp and suspicious, and Lily was sure that the woman's mouth hadn't been open before, or her teeth so pointed.

Then all at once the expression died out of the stone features, as though the spell had given up. With a dull click the other hand slid out of the carved wall, and in it was a heavy golden key, glittering with a cold, unpleasant magic.

'It won't hurt you if I take it?' Lily asked, looking worriedly at the princess's pained face.

She shook her head. 'No. It finishes the spell. Quickly, Lily, please!'

Lily seized the key, expecting it to burn her skin, or bite her, but it was just a key. 'Are you all right?' she asked the princess, who was leaning wearily against the wall. 'What did it do?'

'It was trying to see who I was,' she explained. 'I couldn't tell it – not clearly enough. After all those years at Fell Hall, you see, where they made me think I was mad, and not a princess at all.' She shook herself and stood up straight, tucking her hair neatly inside the hood of her cloak again. 'Quick, Lily. The lock is on her belt, look, that carved clasp.'

Lily nodded, seeing the keyhole now, the dark shape gaping. She pushed the key in, and turned it easily. Then, with a sucking gasp of stale air, a door swung open, the woman's figure disappearing into the darkness.

'Go quietly,' the princess murmured. 'There may be guards, but they should only have spells like the ones used at Fell Hall. No magic of their own. There's a staircase just inside the door; don't fall.'

Lily had expected Archgate to be dark and gloomy – it was a prison, after all. And it was underground. But once they stepped inside the door, she saw that white light was spilling up the staircase, glowing on the stone treads. They were hardly worn at all, and the place was silent. Lily shivered, thinking of the prisoners, abandoned and alone at the bottom of the stairs.

'How many prisoners are there?' she asked. She hadn't even thought about it before – they had only been thinking of their father. 'Are we going to let them all out?'

'There were only ever one or two,' Princess Jane murmured, treading carefully down the stone steps. 'Though more now, perhaps. I suppose it depends who they are.'

'Are there any spells?' Georgie asked nervously, as they reached the last step. 'Can you feel any?'

'Only my own,' Rose said thoughtfully. 'No, don't step down!' She caught Lily's shoulder, yanking her back so that she sat down on the stone step with a thud.

'Oh!' Lily gasped as a huge black dog seemed to leap at her out of the white brightness of the stone passage. It had a lot of teeth, and cold green eyes, and it had come awfully close before it snapped its jaws on nothing and disappeared. 'Was – was that one of yours?'

Rose helped her up. 'Yes. I was rather proud of that one. The guards would never see it, of course. They carry protection against all the spells, embedded into their keys.' She sighed. 'And they were embedded into the prisoners' chains, as well. Stay behind me – I do know where the spells are, but it was a long time ago. I didn't remember that one being so close to the steps. They do shift, over time. And grow…'

Lily could feel Henrietta pressing close against her boots – the spell dog had been extremely large. Lily picked her up, feeling the little dog's heart racing against her fingers. They went on in a line after Rose, creeping down the eerie passageway, now lined with heavy, locked doors.

'How do we know which cell is Father's?' Georgie whispered. 'Are there prisoners behind all these doors?'

Rose stretched out her fingers, beckoning strangely, and on the polished metal door they were passing a figure shimmered and grew. An old woman, much older than Rose herself, with wild, angry eyes. She was staring at them, grinding her teeth.

'Not your father,' Rose muttered. 'And I don't think we should let her out.'

'How did you do that?' Lily asked curiously. 'I made pictures like that, back at home – that's how I got Henrietta. But I had to draw them.'

'Magic often starts in pictures,' Rose told her, staring ahead. 'My own magic began that way, back at the orphanage. Anything shiny... Stop!'

They halted behind her, clutching anxiously at each other and trying to see what it was that Rose could see ahead of them.

'These other cells are empty. But there's something ahead of us, round this corner. Something new. A spell that I had nothing to do with, though it does have something familiar about it.' She frowned. 'They must have wanted an extra layer of protection...'

They rounded the corner of the passage cautiously, piling up behind Rose and peering past her.

'That's a dolls' house!' Georgie said, laughing with relief. Then she swallowed nervously. 'That isn't good, is it? It isn't there for people to play with. I just always wanted a dolls' house like that, it's beautiful.' She looked up at Rose anxiously. 'What have they made it into?'

But Rose wasn't listening to her. She had caught the princess's hand, and they were staring at the dolls' house like two little girls.

'Is that what I think it is?' Rose asked huskily.

Jane nodded. 'I suppose there weren't any children in the palace any more. Mama always hated waste!' She let out a strange sobbing laugh.

'Was it *yours*?' Lily asked curiously.

Princess Jane glanced back at her. 'Yes… Although I stopped playing with it and my little sister Charlotte took it over.'

'Why wouldn't you want to play with it?' Georgie sighed. 'It's perfect.'

Lily nodded. She had never seen a toy like it. It was like a little palace, with its classical front. She guessed it must have at least twenty rooms. Every window had curtains, and on either side of the door were pretty little miniature bay trees.

'I was imprisoned in it.' Jane stepped a little closer. 'I was kidnapped by two magicians – that was how Rose and I met; she was guarding me from another attack. When they struck again, no one had any idea how they'd taken me out of the palace. But it turned out they hadn't at all. They turned me into a doll and shut me away in my own dolls' house. After that, I couldn't seem to want to play with it in the same way…'

'Be careful,' Rose murmured. 'Don't touch it, it's bespelled.'

'Have they done the same thing to the prisoners?' Lily

asked, gazing at the pretty white house in disgust. 'Are they dolls, shut up in there?'

'I don't know…' Rose said thoughtfully. 'I suspect not, though. They'd be easy to look after, but one couldn't speak to them – they'd be useless for information. And you said your father had sent letters, didn't you?'

'Yes!' Lily agreed, in relief. 'You're right, he can't be inside it. But what *is* it for, then?'

Gus prowled along the front of the toy house, sniffing delicately, his whiskers shooting out little glittering sparks. 'It feels to me like just another sort of key spell,' he reported. 'There must be some simple answer to it – it blocks the whole passageway, so the guards must be able to deal with it easily enough.'

'There is a keyhole in the front door,' Georgie suggested doubtfully. 'Perhaps there's a key?'

Rose frowned. 'If it's one of the key spells that they carry around with them, then we're stuck. We'll have to break the lock, which is probably going to be difficult.'

'And incredibly dangerous,' Gus agreed chattily. 'Likely to be fatal, in fact.'

Lily crouched in front of the house, frowning. 'But you helped to create those key spells. You said you'd put an – an antidote to that horrible dog in them. Would it be difficult to add another spell?'

'Yes. But not impossible. I do see what you mean, though. They'd have been more likely to make something new.' Rose stared vaguely around the walls of the passage. 'Something here.'

'Something like this.' Gus darted suddenly under the low table the house was sitting on, and came out purring smugly, with a small, dusty brown thing dangling from his mouth. He seemed to have suddenly grown a fat brown moustache, Lily thought, confused, and then she giggled. A mouse-tache...

'For heaven's sake,' Henrietta growled. 'Cats! Is now really the time?'

'Shut up.' Gus's snarl came out muffled by mouse. 'Look at it! It'th got a collar!'

Henrietta blinked irritably and sidled forward. 'It has,' she admitted. 'With a key on it. That's a very fat mouse.'

'It'th tame.' Gus spat it out, pinning it with one meaty paw. 'Trained to come for food, I should think.'

'But that's not even a spell.' Lily felt rather disappointed. She had wanted something cleverer.

'You think it's too simple?' Rose asked her, looking thoughtfully at the house.

Lily looked at her boots and shrugged. 'I'm probably just being silly.'

'You've come a long way with that sort of instinct,

though…' Rose told her, leaning closer to peer in at the windows. 'Perhaps you're right. But the guards obviously do unlock the door – that mouse is so plump, it must be fed every day. We just need to take the collar off it to use the key. Oh, let it up, Gus.' She took the fat mouse into her hands, staring down at it, and it stared back at her, trembling. 'The poor little thing might never have seen a cat. Oh.' She put the mouse down, rather quickly, on the doorstep of the dolls' house.

'What is it?' Gus asked her sharply.

'That isn't a mouse.'

The cat glared at her. 'It most certainly is. I should know.'

'It's a mouse on the outside, that's all.'

'What is it inside, then?' Lily asked, studying the soft grey-brown fur and the dark, bead-like eyes.

'Something very unpleasant that's been borrowed from somewhere else. Using a spell that no one should teach you until you're much, much older.' Rose sighed. 'Of course, look. Two mice.'

An equally fat mouse had strolled out from under the table, with a matching collar. But this mouse was white. It would be impossible to mistake one for the other if you knew the secret.

'Well done, Lily.' Rose reached out a hand to the white mouse, and carefully unhooked the tiny brass key from its red leather collar. As she reached down to the door of the dolls' house, the brown mouse leaped away from the doorstep, and Lily saw its eyes glittering with a most unmouselike malice. Rose was right – it was no mouse at all.

As the key slid into the lock the whole house seemed to hinge in two, and Lily gasped as it swirled up and around them, the enchanted rooms spinning around their heads, the dolls seeming to lean out and gape at their visitors.

And then it was closed again, quiet and neat and smug-looking – and it was behind them.

TEN

'Oh…' Lily murmured, drawn forward by a strange tugging inside her, something she'd never felt before. She turned back to seize Georgie's hand, and noticed Henrietta trotting eagerly down the passage. 'Can you feel it too?'

The black pug glanced up at her. 'Yes. He's here.'

'Waiting for us!' Georgie was smiling, looking happier than Lily had seen her in weeks. 'I know it! We're coming!' she called, starting to run.

'Georgie, wait!' Lily grabbed her cloak. 'Be careful; we don't know what else is here. There could be more spells.'

Georgie stared longingly down the white passageway, pulling against Lily's grip. Then all at once she slumped back with a sigh, slipping her hand into Lily's. 'You're right. I just want to see him so much. You don't remember…'

Now that they were close to their father, Lily could tell how desperate Georgie was. Not to have him rescue her from the magic that was poisoning her from the inside, but just to be with him again. Lily couldn't remember him at all, and she'd only known their mother as a distant figure, one to be avoided at all costs. But Mama had ruled Georgie with a careful mixture of love and threats, and it had worked cruelly well. She longed for a mother or a father now.

Rose paced forward carefully. 'I think that may have been the last spell,' she said, frowning and reaching her fingers out in front of her, feeling the air. 'Now we just have to unlock the cell door.'

'That one,' Georgie told her eagerly, pointing to a heavy, metal door that faced them at the end of the passage. 'I can tell.'

Lily nodded. 'Why doesn't he call to us?' she whispered to Rose. 'I know it's a heavy door, but I can't hear him at all. He must know we're here.'

Rose gave her a quick warning glance, but Georgie had already turned back to look at them, her eyes wide with fear. 'You think there's something the matter with him?'

Rose sighed. 'How long has he been here?'

'I'm not sure exactly. Nine years?' Georgie frowned thoughtfully at Lily. 'Yes. From when Lily was tiny.'

'Nine years here…' Lily shuddered.

'Exactly. Georgie, he may not be how you remember him,' Rose told her gently, as she walked towards the door.

'I know,' Georgie whispered. 'Let's hurry. He's waiting for us, I'm sure.'

They all stared at the door cautiously, wondering where to begin.

In the end, Lily gave up being patient and careful. She stroked one hand down the heavy door, hearing the hiss of indrawn breath as the others watched her anxiously. She could feel magic seething inside the metal, the power rushing towards her touch. She snatched it away quickly, but not before she'd felt something else behind the door. A curious, friendly, adventurous magic that she was sure was her father's.

'The door's got the same sort of spells they used at Fell Hall, but cast into the metal,' she told the others. 'Spells to squash down people's magic. And they're stronger, more alive. Maybe metal holds magic better than those little glass bottles.'

'It does,' Rose agreed. 'Though they may just have used stronger ones to start with. They had no idea how powerful you young magicians could be. But these are enemies of the state they've got shut up in here. They'll have made them as impenetrable as they can.'

'So you didn't cast these?' Georgie asked anxiously, joining Lily at the door and pressing her fingertips into the buttery shine of the metal.

'No... Only the guard spells.' Rose frowned. 'I don't know who they got to make the building itself. It's a mixture – real stonework and magical building, tied together so closely. I've never seen anything like these doors before.'

'We need Argent...' Lily said, frowning. 'He took those spells off Georgie and all the other children.'

'You don't,' Henrietta snapped. 'He wouldn't fit, for a start. And I have been your familiar for months now. We can do this ourselves. Georgie has been under these spells before, and so has she.' The pug dog nodded her head towards the princess, and Lily cast Princess Jane an apologetic look. Henrietta was always very strict about Lily's manners, but she didn't think the same rules applied to her. 'You managed to ward off the spells at Fell Hall – you never went under. So between you all you ought to know how to get rid of them again.'

The princess nodded, holding out her hands to Lily. 'Can you see inside me? Can you feel where the spells were?'

'Try it, Lily,' Rose agreed. 'Jane is probably safer than Georgie. It's best not to go picking around inside you until we're ready,' she told Georgie apologetically.

Lily took one of Jane's hands and cautiously placed her other hand flat against the door, waiting for the magic to swirl around her again. It was a mist, a thick, heavy fog that rushed into her blood, slowing and subduing her. She shook her head crossly and slammed it away, tearing her fingers from the door. 'No!'

'It's strong, then.' Rose frowned. 'Perhaps we should…'

'I can do it,' Lily snarled crossly. She caught both Jane's hands this time, sending her magic flooding through the old lady's papery skin, searching for the places the deadening magic had lurked inside her.

Slow down. Gently…

She thought it was Rose at first, and then Georgie, talking inside her head the way she had on board the ship. But then she knew.

It was her father, speaking to her for the first time.

Be careful not to hurt her. She's already fragile. Around her memories, I think. And then, more faintly: *Are you really here? I can't tell. Is it just another dream?*

Lily gritted her teeth and pressed her fingers gently against the princess's bony hands, sending her magic deep inside.

A serious little girl sat sewing on a gold brocade chair, watching a younger child dancing up and down with a handful of sugared flowers. She'd eaten too many, and she was going to be sick, Jane was sure. But no one ever listened to her – Charlotte could always wheedle more sweets out of Mama, or the ladies-in-waiting.

The scene was greyish around the edges and slightly wavering, as though its owner was doubtful about it. Lily wasn't sure if that was just age, or if it was the result of the spells. Wouldn't memories fade anyway as one drew further away? But the greyish cast that seeped through the gilded room was a spell, she was sure. A nasty, doubtful, tricksy mist of magic. Lily clawed at it, and felt Princess Jane's fingers tighten on hers. She opened her eyes, suddenly frightened that she'd hurt the old lady.

'Oh, Lily, do that again! I thought Argent had taken all the spells away but that was like someone cleaning a window – suddenly everything was brighter.' The princess stared at her pleadingly.

Lily closed her eyes and concentrated, clawing and pulling away all the dirty mist she could find. The princess sighed happily, leaning against Rose's shoulder, and Lily let go of her hands. She knelt down in front of the door, with Henrietta pressed close to her side. 'Georgie, stand here with me. I felt Father when I touched the door, I'm sure I did. He spoke to me.

*   189   *

I think I understand this spell now, or almost. Enough to try and work against it, anyway.'

'We'll watch you.' Gus patted one soft paw against her hand. 'We'll pull you away if we think you're in any danger.' He touched his whiskers against Henrietta's, a gentle little brush that left a golden shimmer floating in the dusty air around them.

Lily laid her hands back against the door, hating the way it seemed to pull and suck eagerly at her fingers. The metal was so soft, so yielding. It wanted her. Feathery grey wisps were already dusting themselves all through her, wrapping her tightly, pulling her down...

'Lily, shake it off!' Henrietta snapped, shoving her elbow, and Lily drew in a sharp, angry breath, dragging her magic out of the misty softness.

'It's so strong,' she muttered grimly, pressing her nails sharply into the metal again.

Then she gasped. On the other side of the door she could feel fingers pressing back. Hopeful fingers, reaching for hers. Not part of the spell, but someone else working with her against the blanket of grey magic.

'He's there,' she told Georgie excitedly. 'I can feel him working against the spell from his side!'

Georgie hugged her tightly, and suddenly Lily could feel Georgie's strength added to hers. Not the magic that she'd had to leave frozen inside her, but Georgie's love for her little sister, and her desperate wish for a family for them both.

She pushed her hand further through the door, the magic in the metal giving against her fingers. 'Come on,' she hissed, stretching as far as she could, and feeling the spells fighting back against her. Silent, silken webs were wrapping themselves around her, making it hard to breathe. But if she could only reach a little further…

Suddenly, warm fingers touched her own, and caught, sending a huge rush of power into her, so strong that she fell backwards with a squeak, hitting her head against the floor of the passage.

The grey magic caught her at once, swirling triumphantly over and under and around and through her until Lily couldn't find herself. She'd gone. She wasn't herself any more, just a thin grey wispy thing, and she couldn't see.

Then someone shook her, brushing the greyness away like a cobweb, and they were all there, staring down at her. Georgie, and Henrietta, her eyes bulging more than ever. And a man she didn't recognise, but wished she did, with her own wild curly brown hair. Her father.

'It almost had you,' Henrietta said anxiously. 'Lily, are you there? Talk!'

'It's all right. It's gone. What did you do with it?' Lily murmured.

'He did it.' Georgie nodded at the man. 'The door disappeared, and he was there, and he dragged the magic out of you, Lily, and tore it up. Into shreds, horrible little grey shreds, Lily, I saw it.'

I rescued you, but only after you'd rescued me. He was smiling down at her, and his eyes were like hers too, she could see now. He picked her up, setting her gently on her feet. *We should go. The guards aren't due for a while, but someone will have noticed that. Could you tell the others? I – I can't speak.*

Oh! Lily nodded. 'He says we should go, before the guards come.'

Georgie blinked in surprise, but she nodded, and smiled up at their father as he took her hand, hurrying them down the passage towards the stairs.

Too late. They're coming.

'How do you know?' Lily asked him, her voice sharp with fear. The grey magic had left her feeling shaky and weak – she wasn't sure she could fight again.

He pointed ahead, and she saw that the dolls' house was starting to shimmer and swirl apart – someone had unlocked it from the other side.

This time the house disappeared, leaving the passageway open. Standing there were a group of men in the familiar black uniforms, their silver buttons gleaming. But in the middle of them was a tall, white-haired woman who looked very like their own Princess Jane. Lily glanced between the two of them – the faces were so similar. It was only the way the skin was stretched over the bones that made them different – the same nose but sharper, the lips thinner. And the blue eyes furious.

'How could you?' Queen Adelaide snarled. 'Have you no decency? No loyalty? How could you betray us like this?'

'You locked her up! Your guards spent years convincing her she was mad!' Rose yelled, as Jane clung to her. 'How dare you criticise *her*?'

Queen Adelaide was practically spitting with disgust. 'I don't know why you've come back now. This country was a great deal cleaner without your sort. Traitorous scum.'

Lily gasped. She knew that people thought of magicians that way, and they'd heard it at Fell Hall, but it sounded worse coming from someone in a black satin evening dress and an actual crown. Even if it was only a little one.

'Get us out of here,' Gus was hissing, weaving his way round Rose's ankles. 'Look at the guards. They've got more of those spells.'

It was true. Lily could see that all of the Queen's Men were undoing metal canisters that hung from their belts.

Magic was seething out of them, a bluish, ugly vapour that was already making the inside of her nose burn.

Lily, darling, I can't help you. My magic's still weakened by all the spells they've fed me over the years. You girls will have to get us away.

Lily nodded, but she could feel that the door spells had worn her own magic down. It was still there, but only the tiniest spark. No matter how hard she tried to pull it into her skin, it wouldn't flare up the way she needed it to now.

Rose was standing in front of them, Gus still circling around her feet, the touch of his silken fur clearly strengthening her. She was drawing tiny circles with her fingertips; Lily could see them in the air. It rippled like water – she was building a shield, to stop the guards' magic reaching them. But there were at least ten guards, and the magic they were building up together looked strong, even if it wasn't their own.

It wasn't going to work, Lily could see that now. They would all be stuffed back into that cell, for who knew how many years. She couldn't let that happen again.

ARGENT! she screamed silently. He had said that they should call him. He had been furious that they hadn't before, at the palace. Lily didn't know what he would do, how he would reach them. But she was almost sure he would.

And he came. She could feel him coming, the rush of wings beating, the fury and determination as he tore at the stonework with his massive claws, gouging lumps out of the staircase and forcing himself underground again. He came on in a silvery rush, roaring, and for the first time, spouting real flame. It poured down the passageway, blue-white and lethal, sending the Queen's Men scrambling to barricade their mistress inside an empty cell.

The Queen Regent screamed, fighting them, cursing her guards for cowards and ordering them to seize Princess Jane. But they slammed the door, and her voice was muffled and tiny behind the metal.

'Look!' Georgie gasped, her voice choked with dust and smoke. 'On his back!'

Lily peered upward, past the dragon, who was anxiously coiling his neck around them all, trying to see if they were in one piece.

Crouched on the dragon's back, holding on so tightly his hands were white, was a scruffy-looking boy. 'Peter! You came to get us!'

Peter shrugged, as though to say he'd just been passing, and stretched one hand down to haul her up.

Lily clambered up behind him, and reached down for her father's hand.

He was shaking his head, as though he wasn't sure

what he was seeing, and Lily laughed to herself. She had almost forgotten to be amazed about dragons. 'Argent, this is my father,' she told the dragon proudly, as she pulled him up onto the dragon's back.

'Ah. Good. A successful mission then. Though I should have come with you to start with, Lily, quite clearly. But luckily the boy could tell me where to go. Too many twisty little streets for me to follow you. The boy was quite determined that he should come too, and he draws a good map, I'll give him that. Shall we go, then? Is everyone here?'

Lily turned round to see. Her father. Georgie. Rose. The princess. Henrietta and Gus, who'd ended up next to each other, and were pretending that they weren't. And in front of her, his eyes brighter than she'd seen them in weeks, Peter, crooning wordless encouragement to the enormous dragon. 'Yes.' She smiled, feeling her father's arm around her waist. 'We are. We're all here.'

If you liked this story, you'll love...

Lily
and the Traitors' Spell

Turn the page for a sneak peek!

ONE

The bullet buried itself in the canvas backdrop with a solid thud.

Henrietta let out a yelp of surprise, flattening herself against the floor of the stage, with her black eyes bulging.

'It's not meant to have proper bullets in it!' Lily gasped, turning to stare at Daniel, her fingernails digging into her palms.

It had been so quick. If the bullet had been about to hit one of her friends, she wasn't sure she would have been fast enough to stop it.

Argent, who had been sleeping draped across the back of the stage, shook out his wings a little, and blew out a thin, coiling breath of smoke. 'I have little experience with firearms,' he said, in a low, rumbling murmur. 'But that seemed quite real to me.'

Daniel was looking at the pistol, with a faintly puzzled expression on his face. 'It can't have been…'

'I hate this trick,' Nicholas muttered. He and Mary had only been working as Daniel's assistants in the illusionist's act for a few weeks, since they all returned from Fell Hall, but Nicholas swore to Lily that he had nearly died twice. Lily thought he was exaggerating, but perhaps not very much. Nicholas was ideal for the assistant's role, being very skinny and good at getting into tight places, but he had an awful memory, and that mattered when one had to be sure in which order very sharp knives were going to be stabbed through the cabinet one was hiding in. Nicholas had been trying to magic himself a sort of metal vest. He said it wasn't cheating, as the magic wasn't part of the trick, but no one else was convinced. Mary found it particularly irritating, as she had no magic of her own, and had to rely on getting it right the first time.

'Have you been messing with the pistol?' Lily asked Nicholas suspiciously.

Mary glared at him. 'I bet you have!'

'I didn't!' Nicholas protested indignantly. 'I honestly didn't! It isn't fair. Just because of that accidental green rabbit-creature, everyone always blames me.'

Daniel sat down rather shakily on the edge of the stage, laying the ornate enamelled pistol down next to him. 'The rabbit still has a green tinge, Nicholas. And she's really gone off carrots. I don't like putting my hand in that hat any more, she bites.' He sighed. 'That wasn't a wax bullet, was it? What happened?'

Lily came and sat down by him, and Henrietta climbed shakily into her lap, one paw stretched across to Daniel's leg.

'I don't think this trick is a good idea,' Lily muttered. 'This time you were only testing the gun, but what if it happens again?'

'It won't.' Daniel tried to sound reassuring, but it didn't work very well. 'There must have been some sort of mix-up.'

Mary crouched down next to them. 'If that happened when I was firing it at you, I'd never forgive myself. And I don't see why this trick is so special anyway. It's stupid! Who would actually *want* to catch a bullet in their teeth?'

'But if it worked…' Daniel murmured wistfully. 'It's so dramatic…'

'It is quite dramatic when the back of your head is spread all over the stage, yes,' Henrietta growled.

Daniel got up, fetching the shallow box from the top of one of the cabinets. He lifted the lid with shaky fingers, and nudged the glistening black bullets, nicking them with his fingernails. 'These are real. All of them, apart from this one at the end.' He lifted it out, rolling it between his fingers. Then he pressed his forefinger to his lips. 'Sweet. And it isn't as heavy as the others. This is a sugar one, as they all should be.'

'Mystery solved, then,' Henrietta snapped. 'Someone ate your sugar-coated bullets. One of the children.' She glared around at Nicholas suspiciously.

Daniel frowned. 'They aren't all sugar. Just a sugar coat over the wax – baked sugar, to look like metal, you know.'

Argent shook his wings with an anxious rattling sound, and came a little closer, stepping sinuously across the stage. 'Ah… The silvery-black things? The odd sweets, with the rather dull centre?'

Everyone turned to stare up at him, and he ducked his head, looking as embarrassed as a house-sized dragon possibly could. 'I do so like sweet things,' he murmured. 'So much nicer now than marchpane, and liquorice root… I could smell them – so delicious, and the colour so nice. I did put some of the others back in the little box; there was a bag, full of them…'

'Yes,' Daniel agreed grimly. 'The real bullets, for showing to the audience.'

'Ah…'

'I should have noticed, when I loaded it,' Daniel

muttered to himself. 'Perhaps we aren't ready for the gun trick – but it would get us so much publicity.'

'Banner headline. Tragic death of foolish illusionist,' Henrietta muttered.

'I really do apologise,' the dragon said, a flutey, breathless note sounding in his deep voice. 'I shouldn't have taken them. At least it was me that the bullet almost hit, in the end,' he added, snaking his neck down so that he could look up into Daniel's face. 'I'm sorry,' he said again, breathing out a gentle cloud of sparkling, filmy magic that wreathed itself around Daniel's face and shoulders like smoke.

Daniel sighed, and then took a breath in, shivering slightly as the magic shimmered through him, sending a silvery sheen across his skin. 'What did you do?' he murmured. He shook his too-long dark hair a little, as though he were shaking it out of his eyes, and it glittered. 'I feel stronger.'

'Mmm,' Argent agreed. 'It should last a while. I wanted to make it up to you. I should never have eaten them. But I have my doubts about this illusion, Daniel, my friend. Those thugs in the Queen's Men will never believe it's only a trick. Who could catch a bullet in their teeth *without* magic? They'll haul you off to prison – or they would if they had one, anyway.'

He allowed himself a smug little puff of smoke there.

Lily and Georgie had broken into Archgate, the magicians' prison, with help from Princess Jane, whose royal blood could open the locks, and Rose, one of the magicians who had set the original guardian spells. But the Queen's Men had caught them, just as they had managed to rescue their father from the cell he'd been shut in for nearly ten years. Queen Adelaide, the dowager queen, hated all magic and magicians, after a magician had murdered her husband. She had been so determined to see them caught that she'd accompanied the guards to the prison, and she'd ordered her men to kill them all. When she woke in the night, Lily could still hear the old queen's hoarse, delighted voice, screaming gleeful orders as she saw what she had caught.

But Argent had clawed and wrestled his way down the narrow passages and into the heart of the prison to rescue them. The guard spells had no effect on him at all – in fact Lily thought they'd made him stronger. She was almost certain that somehow he ate magic. Which was good, as she wasn't sure what else he ate, and she didn't really want to know.

The prison had been left less than secure. The Queen's Men had put it about that a gang of renegade magicians had attacked the palace, as Archgate was hidden under the ceremonial arch that led into the palace courtyards. Lily had read out the newspaper articles about it to Argent, with disgusted comments, until he had pointed out that actually, she *was* a renegade magician, and now that she had Rose, and her father, as well as Georgie and himself, and Nicholas, however accident-prone his magic was, they were almost a gang.

Lily quite liked the idea.

Lily peered around the door, trying to see into the dark little room. Her father was asleep in there, on a pile of quilts and blankets. Or she'd thought he was. If she hadn't known, she would have sworn the room was empty.

She took a step backwards. The room *was* empty. She shouldn't be there, anyway... Blindly, she turned away from the door, and tripped over Henrietta, who was sitting in the middle of the passageway, shaking her head crossly, as though her ears were itching.

Lily yelped and stumbled, putting her hands out to try to keep from falling onto the dusty floor, and then let out a little gasp of relief as someone caught her with a grunt.

'Peter!'

He shoved her back onto her feet, holding her arms above the elbows and frowning, as though he wasn't sure what had happened.

'I just stumbled – I tripped over Henrietta,' Lily said slowly, but she was staring at the dark doorway as she spoke. That wasn't right… And where had Peter come from, just at the right time to catch her?

Moving in a sort of daze, she turned back to peer at the darkened doorway, stretching an arm across the opening.

Empty. Empty. Empty.

But it *wasn't*. She knew it wasn't. Slowly, as if she was swimming through a golden, sticky syrup, Lily raised the back of her hand to her mouth and bit down hard on her knuckle. The sharp little pain cleared the sticky honey trails out of her head, enough to make her see what was happening.

'You were in there!' she told Peter accusingly, speaking loudly, her face pressed close up against his so he couldn't fail to understand her. 'What were you doing? That's my father's room!'

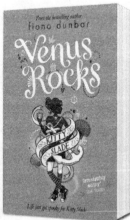